SAFE AND SOUND

LANTERN BEACH GUARDIANS, BOOK 3

CHRISTY BARRITT

COMPLETE BOOK LIST

Squeaky Clean Mysteries:

#1 Hazardous Duty

#2 Suspicious Minds

#2.5 It Came Upon a Midnight Crime (novella)

#3 Organized Grime

#4 Dirty Deeds

#5 The Scum of All Fears

#6 To Love, Honor and Perish

#7 Mucky Streak

#8 Foul Play

#9 Broom & Gloom

#10 Dust and Obey

#11 Thrill Squeaker

#11.5 Swept Away (novella)

#12 Cunning Attractions

#13 Cold Case: Clean Getaway

#14 Cold Case: Clean Sweep

#15 Cold Case: Clean Break

#16 Cleans to an End

While You Were Sweeping, A Riley Thomas Spinoff

The Sierra Files:

#1 Pounced

#2 Hunted

#3 Pranced

#4 Rattled

The Gabby St. Claire Diaries (a Tween Mystery series):

The Curtain Call Caper

The Disappearing Dog Dilemma

The Bungled Bike Burglaries

The Worst Detective Ever

#1 Ready to Fumble

#2 Reign of Error

#3 Safety in Blunders

#4 Join the Flub

#5 Blooper Freak

#6 Flaw Abiding Citizen

#7 Gaffe Out Loud

#8 Joke and Dagger

#9 Wreck the Halls

#10 Glitch and Famous

Raven Remington

Relentless 1

Relentless 2 (coming soon)

Holly Anna Paladin Mysteries:

#1 Random Acts of Murder

#2 Random Acts of Deceit

#2.5 Random Acts of Scrooge

#3 Random Acts of Malice

#4 Random Acts of Greed

#5 Random Acts of Fraud

#6 Random Acts of Outrage

#7 Random Acts of Iniquity

Lantern Beach Mysteries

#1 Hidden Currents

#2 Flood Watch

#3 Storm Surge

#4 Dangerous Waters

#5 Perilous Riptide

#6 Deadly Undertow

Lantern Beach Romantic Suspense
Tides of Deception
Shadow of Intrigue
Storm of Doubt
Winds of Danger
Rains of Remorse
Torrents of Fear

Lantern Beach P.D.
On the Lookout
Attempt to Locate
First Degree Murder
Dead on Arrival
Plan of Action

Lantern Beach Escape
Afterglow (a novelette)

Lantern Beach Blackout
Dark Water
Safe Harbor
Ripple Effect
Rising Tide

Lantern Beach Guardians

Hide and Seek

Shock and Awe

Safe and Sound

Lantern Beach Blackout: The New Recruits

Rocco (coming soon)

Crime á la Mode

Deadman's Float

Milkshake Up

Bomb Pop Threat

Banana Split Personalities

The Sidekick's Survival Guide

The Art of Eavesdropping

The Perks of Meddling

The Exercise of Interfering

The Practice of Prying

The Skill of Snooping

The Craft of Being Covert

Saltwater Cowboys

Saltwater Cowboy

Breakwater Protector

Cape Corral Keeper

Seagrass Secrets

Driftwood Danger

Carolina Moon Series

Home Before Dark

Gone By Dark

Wait Until Dark

Light the Dark

Taken By Dark

Suburban Sleuth Mysteries:

Death of the Couch Potato's Wife

Fog Lake Suspense:

Edge of Peril

Margin of Error

Brink of Danger

Line of Duty

Cape Thomas Series:

Dubiosity

Disillusioned

Distorted

Standalone Romantic Mystery:

The Good Girl

Suspense:
Imperfect
The Wrecking

Sweet Christmas Novella:
Home to Chestnut Grove

Standalone Romantic-Suspense:
Keeping Guard
The Last Target
Race Against Time
Ricochet
Key Witness
Lifeline
High-Stakes Holiday Reunion
Desperate Measures
Hidden Agenda
Mountain Hideaway
Dark Harbor
Shadow of Suspicion
The Baby Assignment
The Cradle Conspiracy
Trained to Defend
Mountain Survival

Nonfiction:

Characters in the Kitchen

Changed: True Stories of Finding God through Christian Music (out of print)

The Novel in Me: The Beginner's Guide to Writing and Publishing a Novel (out of print)

CHAPTER ONE

THE FOOTSTEPS WERE QUIET.

But they were there.

Behind her.

Traveling through foliage so thick it choked any signs of the early morning sun.

One wrong move could mean the difference between life and death.

Police Chief Cassidy Chambers kept her steps steady as she slipped between gnarled live oaks, prickly underbrush, and moss that draped low-lying branches like fragile shawls.

Her survival instinct urged her to run.

But, if she did, the person following her through the woods would know exactly where she was. Once she made the first move and announced her presence, she would face an all-out fight for her life.

Her pulse pounded in her ears. Leaves whispered as she brushed by them. A bird squawked in the distance, almost as if warning of what she could only sense.

There it was again.

Another footfall.

A stick had cracked under an unseen weight.

Nature had gone silent at the sound.

Even the breeze had died.

As sweat covered her forehead, Cassidy's future flashed through her mind. Ty's face appeared. His handsome face—one she could stare at all day.

How would he take the news if something happened to her?

She should have been expecting this. She'd known it was a possibility that someone would find her. She'd been living on borrowed time for nearly three years now.

She paused and leaned against a tree, trying to control her breath, her pulse. She had to sort her thoughts.

She'd been called out to investigate what sounded like someone calling for help in the woods. A passerby had reported it. Cassidy's other officers were working a 5K race that should be wrapping up any time now.

But she had a feeling this had all been a setup.

There hadn't been anyone out here crying for help.

Someone had wanted Cassidy to come.

Her fingers dug into the rough bark of the tree as she waited. Her other hand held her gun.

It was almost like she was being hunted.

What was she going to do? Call for help?

Her officers wouldn't get here in time.

Keep running?

Even if Cassidy did, there was no safe haven waiting ahead. She'd eventually reach either the street, the ocean, or the lighthouse.

Then she would be totally exposed.

Her police SUV sat on the other side of this patch of forest, in the opposite direction. She couldn't reach it without doubling back.

Or she could stop running and simply fight, she realized.

She just didn't know what—or who—she was facing.

Based on what she heard, only one person followed her.

Ever since someone had discovered Cassidy's

real identity several days ago, she'd been looking over her shoulder. Until then, only Cassidy, her husband, and her friend Mac MacArthur had known the truth.

Because if the wrong person found out, Cassidy was a dead woman.

Since every life affected another, she knew the turmoil wouldn't end if she died. Ty would be affected. He might even become a victim. At the very least, he'd probably want vengeance. Vengeance that could ruin his life.

Footsteps crunched leaves. The noise was followed by what sounded like a grunt.

A grunt?

Her muscles tightened again.

No more running, she realized.

She was only delaying the inevitable.

If she was going to fight, at least she could do it while trees offered cover.

Her heart throbbed as she gripped her gun.

Then, on the count of three, she pushed herself away from the tree. "Come out! I know you're there!"

She waited, her pulse nearly deafening.

Everything went quiet again.

But she remained still, knowing danger could spring on her at any minute.

She held her gun, readying herself to act.

A moment later, a man stepped from the shadows.

Cassidy braced herself for a fight.

CHAPTER TWO

CASSIDY STARED at the man and recoiled as shock coursed through her.

"Samuel?" She whispered the name as she stared at the fifty-something man with the prematurely aging face. The thick salt-and-pepper hair. The fit build.

She lowered her gun slightly.

Certainly, her eyes were tricking her.

That couldn't be her friend. The FBI agent. The one who'd watched over her when she'd taken on her new identity. For the longest time, he was one of the only people she could trust.

And now . . . he was here.

Following her.

But there was more. His eyes . . . they didn't look right.

"Cassidy . . ." He practically croaked out the word.

Her breath caught as he clutched his chest.

Blood spread across his shirt near his heart.

He was hurt. Based on the rips in his shirt, he'd been stabbed.

"Samuel!" She rushed toward him, concern filling her.

Cassidy reached the agent just as he went down on his knees and drew in a raspy, labored breath.

She'd been around death enough to know when it was near . . . peril claimed the air around her now, clutching it with its prickly fingers.

"No . . ." She grabbed Samuel's elbows, trying to catch him before he completely collapsed. "Let me call backup, 911. We can help you."

With surprising strength, Samuel grabbed her wrist and his gaze locked on hers. "No . . . time."

As another realization hit her, Cassidy jerked her head up.

What if the person who'd done this was close? What if he was waiting to strike again?

She scanned the woods.

Trees stared back.

Samuel gasped again.

She swung her gaze back toward him.

No . . .

"Who did this to you?" she rushed, staring at her friend's sullen eyes.

Somehow, she knew it was too late.

Samuel had only minutes left.

What was Samuel even doing here in Lantern Beach? He hadn't been to visit her in person since her death had been faked. Since Cady Matthews had died and been reborn as Cassidy Chambers.

"They . . . know . . ."

She leaned closer, desperate to hear what he said next. "Who knows? What do they know?"

He stared at her another moment before his eyes glazed.

"Samuel? Don't leave. Hang in!" Cassidy grasped his shoulders, trying to keep him lucid.

But she knew it was too late.

Her friend was gone.

____

CHAPTER THREE

TEARS PRESSED at Cassidy's eyes as she stared at Samuel's lifeless body.

She gave herself a moment to mourn before glancing up. Whoever had done this had, at one time, been near.

Where was that person now? Had he watched Samuel draw his last breath? Was he waiting, anticipating his next move?

Her spine straightened as anger surged through her.

Cassidy stood and grasped her gun. She glanced around, searching for the cowardly killer who had done this.

But everything remained silent around her.

Her instincts told her the person who'd attacked him wasn't far away.

But now Cassidy had to figure out what to do—starting with reporting this to the FBI.

Yet reporting it to the FBI would mean questions. They would want to know how Cassidy knew Samuel. Would want to know what he was doing here.

And that meant that Cassidy would need to spill everything about her past. That meant more people would know. That meant life as she knew it would be over.

Yet she couldn't let the person who'd done this to her friend get away with it.

The decision pulled inside her until her head pounded.

She had to do the right thing, she realized. The right thing was to find the person responsible. She didn't want the world to know who she really was. But she couldn't hide this either.

Somehow, Cassidy knew a chapter of her life had just ended.

She knew that a new one was beginning. But she wasn't sure what this new one had in store.

They know.

Samuel's last words echoed in her mind.

What had he meant?

She'd need to figure that out later. For now, she grabbed her phone so she could get this investigation underway.

AN HOUR LATER, Cassidy's officers were on the scene, along with Doc Clemson, the medical examiner and island doctor.

Cassidy had put in a call to the FBI, and they'd told her to preserve the scene but not to touch anything. They wanted their guys to do that. She'd already checked Samuel's pockets, but she'd found nothing of note on him—nothing that gave her any answers.

A perimeter had been put up to ensure nobody could get through. While her guys contained the scene, Cassidy needed to search the woods for any sign of what had happened.

Just as she stepped into the thick forest, she heard footsteps rushing her way.

Ty. Her husband. He was here.

His broad figure filled her gaze, along with his messy, dark hair and striking blue eyes.

Even after two years of marriage, seeing him still made her heart flutter.

Cassidy had called him and asked him to come out. First, he'd had to find someone for Annabeth to stay with.

Annabeth Manchester was the six-year-old girl they'd found on the beach a few weeks ago. She was staying with them until she could go back to live with her parents. The girl had quickly warmed their hearts.

Ty didn't say anything as he joined Cassidy. Instead, he fell into step beside her.

Finally, when the two of them were far away from anyone else, he spoke.

"How are you holding up?" He kept his voice low as the underbrush crunched beneath their feet.

Cassidy stepped over a downed tree covered with moss and fungi. "My mind won't stop racing. What was Samuel even doing here? Who killed him? Why?"

"I wish I could give you some of those answers. It doesn't make sense, does it?"

Cassidy paused and glanced around, double-checking that no one was close. Then she leaned toward Ty. "The even stranger thing? His last words were, 'They know.'"

He narrowed his eyes until they were just slits. "What does that mean?"

She shrugged. "I wish I knew. Was he talking about me? That somebody knows my real identity? And, if so, who is *they*?"

Ty's jaw hardened. "I don't know, and I don't like this. It seems like we get one obstacle out of the way only to hit another, doesn't it?"

She frowned. They couldn't seem to catch a break lately. First, finding a girl washed up from the ocean. Then, discovering the governor was involved. Then finding that girl's mom held captive so master criminals could use her hacking skills to discover secrets about people so they could black-mail them.

Cassidy nodded toward the trail. "We need to keep walking. I don't want anyone to get suspicious."

He followed behind her as she continued to search the woods. "So what are you going to do when the FBI gets here?"

"I have no choice but to tell them, Ty. Whoever did this to Samuel . . . they need to pay. I can't stand in the way of that."

Ty grabbed her arm and pulled her to a stop. "But that would mean . . ."

She pulled her eyes up to meet his, grief trying to

claim her heart. "I know. I know what it means. But I don't know what else to do."

The air seemed to leave his lungs in a low, steady *whoosh*. "Cassidy . . . there has to be another way. Certainly, there are other people with the FBI who know your story."

"Maybe. But I don't know who. And I don't even know who to talk to about the situation."

"Just don't make any knee-jerk reactions. We need to think this through."

Before she could respond, she looked down.

Blood stained the underbrush beneath her.

She knelt to get a better look before muttering, "This is where it happened. This is where someone stabbed Samuel."

As she said the words, anger heated her blood.

Whoever did this would not get away with it.

Cassidy would make sure of that.

CHAPTER FOUR

TY BRISTLED as he glanced around the dense maritime forest surrounding him.

Someone had killed Samuel in cold blood. That person was still out there. Still lurking. Still a danger.

He appreciated Cassidy's stance on finding justice, even if it meant sacrificing herself.

But that was the last thing he wanted.

There had to be another solution.

Just then, a helicopter whirred overhead.

No doubt, the FBI had arrived.

From what Ty had heard, the team would land in the parking lot near the lighthouse. One of Cassidy's officers would go pick them up and bring them to the scene.

That was when things might start getting ugly.

Cassidy rose after taking several pictures of the blood on the leaves and the ground. "We don't have much time. Come on."

After Cassidy placed a marker at the spot, they both continued through the woods, moving away from the crew who remained with Samuel's body.

Ty hated to think about whatever had played out here.

He didn't think Samuel had been on the wrong side of the law. From what Ty knew about the man, he was an upstanding FBI agent. Without him, Ty and Cassidy wouldn't have been able to live the life they had together.

Ty glanced at Cassidy as she walked in front of him. She studied the ground—for evidence, for footprints. He saw the tension in her shoulders, the stiffness in her neck.

This situation had her on edge—probably more than she'd ever admit.

"Where are you going?" Ty asked.

"I need to figure out where Samuel parked. It couldn't have been too far away. I want to see his car before the FBI does."

"You're not going to look inside, are you?"

A brief moment of indecision flashed through

her gaze before being replaced with a firm head-shake. "No. I can't do that. I don't think Samuel would have left anything in his car about me anyway. He was too smart for that. But I want to see if there are any clues there before the FBI arrives."

"Did you check his pockets?"

"I did. I found his cell phone and wallet. But nothing else."

"They might trace your number through his cell phone."

Cassidy frowned. "I know. I thought about that. But if I mess with the cell phone, then I'm going to jail."

Ty nodded, the action tight and rigid. Because Cassidy was right. She could tell the truth and face those consequences. Or she could try to cover this up and face a different set of consequences. Neither seemed ideal.

"There!" Cassidy pointed to something smooth and shiny in the distance.

A car.

The two of them ran through the woods until they reached it.

A black sedan had been left in the brush on the side of the road.

Most likely, it was Samuel's.

Just as Cassidy stepped toward it, Ty spotted something beneath the vehicle.

A red, flashing light.

His breath caught.

Almost as if in slow motion, he yelled, "No!"

But he feared that it was too late.

CASSIDY HEARD TY YELL.

The next instant, he slammed into her.

They flew across the road and landed on the asphalt with a thud just as a ball of fire filled the air.

Cassidy's heart pounded into her ribcage as she glanced back.

Samuel's car had just exploded.

Not *just* exploded.

The blast had been on purpose. Planned. Maybe someone had even deliberately detonated it right at this moment—right when Cassidy got close.

Did that mean the person was lurking nearby? Watching them?

She doubted it. Most likely, a sensor had been installed.

Ty rolled to his side and studied her, probably looking for any signs of injury. "Are you okay?"

At least, that's what Cassidy thought he said. Her ears rang. Her hair smelled singed by the flames. That's how close she'd been.

A few feet closer and . . . she shuddered. She didn't want to think about it.

She glanced down at her police uniform, quickly checking herself for broken bones, burns, or scrapes. "I'm okay, I think. You?"

Ty pushed himself up more and let out a sigh. "I'll definitely feel this in the morning."

"You and me both. Quick thinking. How did you know?"

"I saw a flashing red light under the car, and I figured something was up."

"I'm glad you did." Cassidy squeezed his arm, grateful for his skills of observation.

They pulled themselves to their feet and brushed off dirt and small pieces of shrapnel from the blast. Cassidy's elbow had been scratched, and she might have a bruise on her hip.

At least they were alive.

She stared at the remains of Samuel's car as the flames still flickered. The vehicle's shell remained. But fire filled the inside, and the scent of burning rubber—from the tires, no doubt—filled the air.

Someone hadn't wanted them to see whatever was inside.

Or someone had wanted to send a message.

Either way, a dangerous game was playing out.

Cassidy called the fire department to come to extinguish this.

Just as she finished making the call, a police car pulled to a stop beside them.

The door opened, and Special Agent Watkins stepped out.

Her last conversation with Samuel slammed back into her mind.

There's something about him that I don't trust.

"What's going on here?" Watkins strode toward them, his face red with premature accusation. He glanced at Ty and his gaze narrowed even further. "And what is he doing here?"

Cassidy bristled again. "The car exploded. Ty is here because he's a former Navy SEAL, a private security agent, and a deputized officer here on the island. Any more questions?"

Watkins didn't miss a beat. "Oh, I have plenty. Starting with, did you touch that car before it exploded?"

Cassidy swallowed hard, wondering exactly where all this was going to lead.

A bad feeling brewed in her gut as she thought about the possibilities.

CHAPTER FIVE

WATKINS GLARED AT TY. "I need a moment alone with your wife."

Ty waited until Cassidy gave him a nod before walking away.

She was a strong woman. She could handle herself. But he hated to think about everything that was about to go down.

Hesitantly, he wandered toward Mac MacArthur, the town's former police chief and current mayor. He'd arrived on the scene a few minutes ago.

Several people stood on the road near where Samuel's body had been found—Cassidy's officers, a couple of paramedics, and Doc Clemson, for starters. A gentle breeze clattered the leaves, and the sun, when it hit between the branches, glared down on them as if demanding its presence be known.

"What's going on?" Mac's voice contained an edge of seriousness that Ty rarely heard in the happy-go-lucky man. Well, happy-go-lucky unless something was going wrong on the island—which seemed to be happening more and more often lately.

Ty filled him in on what he knew. Mac was the only other person here on this island who knew about Cassidy's true past. Cassidy thought of the man like a father, and Ty was certain that Mac thought of Cassidy as the daughter he never had.

"This doesn't make sense." Mac rubbed his short, white beard as he shook his head.

"I know." Ty kept his voice low. "I don't know why Samuel would have risked coming here."

"It had to be important."

"Maybe he was coming to warn her," Ty said. "It's the only thing that makes sense. But why wouldn't he just call her on the phone?"

"Good question," Mac said. "The other question is, who might have discovered her real identity? DH-7? Did they follow Samuel here and kill him? And if that's the case, why didn't they go after Cassidy? Why kill Samuel but let Cassidy go free, especially since she was right out there with him?"

Mac's words left a hollow feeling in Ty's chest. But his friend made some valid points.

"I don't know." Ty rolled his shoulders, his neck stiff and his upper body beginning to ache with tension. "But I don't like this. And Watkins isn't going to make this easier."

Mac's gaze flickered up to his, questions dwelling in the depths of his eyes. "Is Cassidy going to tell them the truth about her past?"

Ty frowned at the thought. He didn't like the idea of it. But how could she not mention it? There would be so many questions if she kept that part of her life secret.

"She's thinking about it," Ty finally said. "She's in a hard spot."

"She's a smart woman. Let's see what she figures out. And then let's be there to support her—whatever happens."

Ty knew Mac's words were true.

He just wanted to make all this better.

And he had no idea how to do that.

CASSIDY CROSSED her arms as she stared at Special Agent Watkins. They stood away from the rest of the crowd and behind an ambulance that had arrived on scene.

Cassidy had met the fed a couple of weeks ago when he'd come into town to investigate a missing FBI agent. The man worked out of the Raleigh field office. He had a square face, light brown hair that he kept short, and if he liked his drinks as strong as his cologne then he was going to have issues.

He wasn't the most personable man, and Cassidy had gotten on his bad side when she'd found a killer and broken a case before he had.

Cassidy remembered his question. *Did you touch that car before it exploded?* "I was staking out all the evidence so I could show you when you arrived."

Watkins narrowed his eyes, obviously not trusting her. "Is that right? I told you not to touch anything."

"And I didn't touch it."

"So how did his car happen to blow up right when you were there?"

"When we approached it, Ty saw the bomb beneath the wheel well—a flashing red light was visible. A few seconds later, an explosion knocked us off our feet. Did you consider that it went off, not because I touched the car, but because somebody had set it off?"

Irritation flickered through his gaze. "That would mean that somebody was close by and watching."

"Exactly."

Watkins continued to stare Cassidy down, almost as if he wanted to intimidate her. "This is the second FBI agent who's died on your island in the past week. What do you have to say about that?"

Cassidy's spine stiffened. She didn't appreciate his tone—or his insinuations. "I don't like it any more than you do."

"Have you ever talked to Samuel Stephens before?" Watkins kept his tone as icy cold as his gaze.

Cassidy swallowed hard, knowing that however she answered would set into motion an irreversible chain of events. She didn't have time to dwell on the possibilities. She had to make a decision. Now.

Finally, she nodded. "Yes, I did know Special Agent Stephens."

"How?"

"The matter is confidential." This was her best option. She needed to buy herself some time, and she hoped her statement would do the trick.

Watkins narrowed his eyes, not bothering to hide his irritation. "I'd say this warrants you being able to share whatever it is."

"Of course, I wish that I could. But I'm legally

bound to stay quiet on the matter until someone higher up clears me to give any details. I'm sorry."

Watkins' face reddened. "Is that right? Because if you're not telling the truth, I'll bring you in for questioning myself. You know that, don't you? I don't take kindly to people trying to pull the wool over my eyes."

Cassidy had no doubt his words were true. In fact, part of her felt like Watkins had it in for her since the moment they'd first met.

She raised her chin. "I'm just trying to follow the letter of the law. I thought you'd appreciate that."

"I only appreciate it when it doesn't get in the way of me solving my cases—especially when it's a friend who's died."

Cassidy held her ground. "I'm going to need approval before I share anything. I know it's not what you want to hear, but that's just the way it is. And Samuel was my friend also. I'm not taking this matter lightly."

Watkins glared, clearly not used to being told no. "Fine. In the meantime, stay out of my investigation. Do you understand?"

Watkins' tone made bile rise in her. Cassidy didn't like this man. She'd tried to give him respect because of his title. But that was getting harder and harder.

"Understood." She forced the word out.

He turned to his guys. "Let's get busy. We need to scour these woods and find any evidence that's been left . . . any evidence that hasn't already been tampered with."

Cassidy heard the accusation in his tone, and her eyes narrowed.

She could feel the walls closing in on her.

And she knew this would get harder before it got any easier.

CHAPTER SIX

"CHIEF, can I have a word with you?"

Cassidy looked away from the scene as she and her officers guarded the perimeter and watched the FBI work.

Officer Dane Bradshaw stared at her. The man was tall with an olive complexion and a friendly smile. But she'd seen Bradshaw looking at her with questions haunting his eyes. The man was intelligent—not that her other officers weren't. But his keen sense of observation seemed more prominent than her other guys.

"Of course," Cassidy finally told him.

After the two of them walked away from everyone else, Bradshaw turned to her. His gaze was hooded and his features tight. "What's going on?"

Cassidy shrugged. "I wish I could tell you more. But the FBI has taken over, and they're being tightlipped."

He continued to study her, scrutiny in his gaze. He knew something wasn't adding up. "Did you find the person who was in trouble out here?"

Cassidy drew in a quick breath. That was right. She'd nearly forgotten the call that had led her here.

She'd been searching for someone who might be lost or hurt—thanks to that good Samaritan who'd called, saying someone needed help out here.

That was when she'd heard someone behind her.

And then the caller had been forgotten.

But if Cassidy had to guess, the distress call wasn't real at all. Someone had simply led her out here. Like a lamb to slaughter? But if that was the case, why hadn't this person killed her when he'd had the chance? He could have used that bomb to do it.

Unrest jostled inside her.

She turned her focus back to Bradshaw, reminding herself that the man was sharp and suspicious. Her acting skills were about to be put to the test. "I'm not sure at all that that call was even real."

"Someone wanted you to come out here?" Bradshaw's intense gaze remained on Cassidy.

"That's how it appeared."

Bradshaw crossed his arms. "Is there something you're not telling us, Chief?"

Cassidy's stomach dropped, although his question shouldn't have surprised her. He was a smart man and a good officer. She'd figured it was only a matter of time before her guys started to ask her probing questions.

She stared up at him and contemplated her words. She didn't like keeping secrets from people. However, anyone who knew would be at risk. That was the last thing that she wanted.

It wouldn't be long before Bradshaw put more things together and asked more questions.

But right now wasn't the time for her to spill everything. Maybe there would never be a right time.

Cassidy shifted, resting her hands on her duty belt. "I found a dead body, and I'm trying to get to the bottom of what happened. But it's complicated. I don't like any of this any more than you do."

He narrowed his gaze. "And that's all?"

She swallowed hard. She couldn't tell him the

whole truth. She'd been living this lie for a long time now, and it never got easier.

"That's all." Her throat burned as she said the words. "I'm hoping the FBI will give us some answers soon."

As soon as she said the words, Watkins started toward her. Based on the way he shot daggers with his gaze, he didn't have good news.

He held up a plastic bag with a cell phone inside it. "Is there a reason why Special Agent Stephens called you last week?"

Cassidy bristled. "I told you, there are some things I'm not free to speak about."

Watkins took her arm. "Fine. We'll do this the hard way. Chief Chambers, I'm officially taking you in for questioning."

She sucked in a quick breath. That had escalated quickly.

Cassidy glanced back at her officers as Watkins led her away. "Stay on the scene, guys, and keep an eye on everything until I get back."

But based on the look of concern on their faces, Bradshaw wasn't going to be the only one questioning what was really going on.

"WHERE'S CASSIDY?" Ty stormed over to Bradshaw and glanced around. But he didn't see his wife anywhere.

Bradshaw's lips flickered down in a frown. "Watkins just took her in. He didn't look happy."

Lava flowed through Ty's veins as he listened to Bradshaw's words. Had he even heard correctly? "He did what?"

Bradshaw nodded. "I don't know what's going on, but it doesn't look good. Is Cassidy involved in this somehow?"

Ty's eyes widened even more. "I'm not sure what you're implying, but certainly you don't think she hurt anyone, do you?"

"I don't want to." Bradshaw's voice held an edge of caution. "There's a lot going on here. A lot of secrets."

"Trust me, Cassidy's only trying to look out for everyone's best interests. You should know her well enough to know that."

Bradshaw rubbed his jaw, almost as if trying to conceal his frown. "That's what I want to believe."

Ty stepped closer. "She needs your support right now more than ever. Give her a chance."

Bradshaw stared at Ty a moment before nodding. "I will."

Ty wanted to track Cassidy down himself. But he knew it was no use. There was no way Watkins would let him near her now, not unless Ty himself was being interrogated.

Where had the man even taken her? Had Watkins taken jurisdiction at the local police station?

This situation was going south, and it was going south fast.

Ty hurried back to his truck.

He would go to the station. Then he'd wait. The first chance he got, Ty would talk to Cassidy, and they'd figure out a plan.

CHAPTER SEVEN

CASSIDY FORCED herself to remain calm and unemotional as she stared at Watkins and his rookie sidekick on the other side of the conference table. The rookie looked to be in his mid-twenties with neat, dark brown hair and a baby face that only made him look too young to be intimidating.

If she remembered correctly, his name was Rohl.

At least the two of them hadn't taken Cassidy into the interrogation room. She'd count her blessings any way she could get them.

"How do you know Samuel Stephens?" Watkins asked.

Cassidy licked her lips as she prepared herself to answer.

"Unfortunately, Samuel didn't tell me who I

could trust with the information that I was given," Cassidy said. "Until I can figure that out, I can't share anything about how Samuel and I know each other."

Watkins narrowed his eyes again and tapped one of his fingers on the glossy tabletop. "You're going to need to do better than that."

She'd already been through everything with Watkins when she'd spoken with him earlier. The reason she'd been out in the woods. How she'd found Samuel.

Watkins didn't seem to believe anything she said. In fact, his skepticism only seemed to grow the more they talked.

Was that because he was dirty? Was he looking for someone to frame for Samuel's death?

Cassidy didn't know.

But she *did* know this was a fight for her survival.

And on top of it all, Watkins had brought Cassidy into her own police station, using one of her own patrol cars, for the interrogation. He wanted to humiliate her, and she didn't take kindly to that fact.

Cassidy leaned closer, knowing she needed to establish some boundaries if she was going to get through this. "If you think you're going to intimidate me into sharing something I'm not at liberty to share, then you're wrong."

"The fact is, whoever killed Stephens had to be skilled. No one could have taken down an agent like Stephens otherwise. You seem like the type of cop who might be smart enough to pull that off."

The breath left her lungs. Watkins was right. Not just any old joe off the street could take an FBI agent by surprise.

That only made things look worse for Cassidy.

Which meant she needed to take this to the next level.

She didn't want to. She wanted to resolve this easily and quickly.

But that didn't seem possible.

Her voice stiffened as she said, "I have the right to an attorney, and I'm going to use that right now."

"Fine." Watkins leaned back, still giving her that cold stare. "Go ahead and make a call. We'll be waiting."

Cassidy took her phone and dialed the number for Ricco Salvatore, one of the lawyers here on the island. The man seemed adept at his job. She was counting on his skills now.

A moment later, she ended the call. Ricco promised to be on his way, and if he left right now, Cassidy knew he could be here in five minutes. That's what she was hoping for.

In the meantime, Watkins scowled at her from across the table. "Stephens was a good FBI agent."

"I thought so too."

He remained silent a moment, his gaze clearly calculating. "How long have you known him?"

He might be trying the more casual approach, but Cassidy wasn't going to fall for it. "No comment."

His jaw shifted, almost as if he gritted his teeth. "You're not doing yourself any favors, you know."

Cassidy said nothing. The man was just trying to get any information out of her that he could. And it wasn't going to work.

Finally, Ricco knocked at the door and his gaze met Cassidy's. "Don't say another word. You and I need to talk."

"THAT SOUNDS like something that would happen in Hollywood," Ricco told her.

They'd gone into Cassidy's office so they could speak privately.

Ricco was now the third person on the island who knew Cassidy's real identity. Because of attorney-client privilege, Cassidy had no choice but to trust him. She knew she couldn't stay silent on these details, not if she wanted to get out of this situation.

Ricco paced the small area in front of her desk. The man was short and thin, but he exuded strength and intelligence. And right now, he was thinking and formulating.

He rubbed his chin and continued to pace. "Is there anybody at the FBI you can talk to?"

"Samuel was my only contact." Cassidy crossed her arms, unable to sit. "I suppose I could try to find out who his superior is."

"Do that. And in the meantime, they have no evidence to hold you. You know that."

"I know." She glanced down and saw a small spot of blood on her arm. She raised it to show him. "But the fact is, I was at the scene, I have no alibi, Samuel's blood is on me, and they found my name and number in his phone along with a record of him calling me last week."

Ricco frowned. "I agree that it might not look good. But until these guys have something more concrete, you should be free to investigate on your own."

"Until they accuse me of impeding a federal investigation."

"You're going to have to watch your steps."

CHAPTER EIGHT

WATKINS HAD no choice but to let Cassidy go.

She knew she had to make some tough choices. But first she needed to talk to Ty about them.

When she stepped from the station, she saw him waiting for her beside his vintage Ford truck. It was like he'd read her mind. She needed him right now, and here he was.

Cassidy climbed in the passenger side and slammed the door.

"I need to have a meeting." She kept her voice low, despite their privacy. "I'd love for the Blackout team to be there as well as my officers."

Ty shifted toward her, concern in his gaze as tension stretched across his broad chest. "What's going on, Cassidy?"

"My hand is being forced. Either I can live in fear and wait for everybody to figure out who I really am." She swallowed hard as she looked up at her husband. "Or I can tell them myself."

He sucked in a sharp breath. "Cassidy . . . what are you talking about?"

"I'm not going to announce my real identity to the world. But if I'm going to get through this, then I'm going to need to tell a few people what's really going on. One of my officers is already starting not to trust me. I can't let that happen. I need them to have my back."

"And Blackout?" He said the words calmly, but Cassidy saw the storm in his gaze.

"I may need a hand from them. I'd rather get my announcement over with all at once and not have to do it multiple times."

Ty stared at her another moment, and Cassidy braced herself for an argument. Maybe even a fight.

Instead, he nodded slowly. "Okay. I'll make it happen."

"Thank you. And Ty . . ." She paused and glanced around, still on guard for anyone listening despite the closed doors. "I can't do the meeting here at the station. FBI agents are going to be in and out. Can we use the Blackout facility?"

"Of course. Give me a few minutes."

"Thanks. I need to call my guys and see if they can meet me there. Most of them are at the crime scene now, but I'm hoping they'll be able to leave soon."

"How about if we meet back in an hour? Is that enough time?"

Cassidy nodded. "If we wait much longer, who knows what the FBI might find."

Ty paused and studied her face, a touch of trepidation lingering in the depths of his eyes. It was almost like he didn't want to know, like he anticipated more bad news. "What does that mean?"

Her stomach squeezed before she said the words, "It means . . . I'm afraid I am being framed."

Ty's eyes widened, but he didn't ask any questions. "Then I better get busy."

He quickly kissed her cheek, his lips lingering against her skin for just a brief moment.

Then Cassidy scrambled from his truck. She didn't have any time to waste.

UNEASE CHURNED in Ty's gut as he stared out his windshield. He hadn't started his truck. Not yet.

He wanted a few seconds to process what Cassidy had just told him.

He didn't like where this was going. He also knew that Cassidy was right.

There was a good chance that she *was* being framed for this. It would explain why some mysterious person had called her to the woods. It would explain why Samuel had been killed but the murderer had fled before coming after Cassidy. It explained why the car had exploded.

Thankfully, all his guys from Blackout were in Lantern Beach right now and not on other missions. And tomorrow, the first of the new recruits would be coming. So today was a perfect day to get this over and done with.

Ty's mind went back to Annabeth.

The girl had been with them for more than three weeks now and was adjusting nicely. But now that they knew her mother was still alive, Ty knew the girl was anxious to be with her mom.

The FBI was still holding Alexandria Manchester, Annabeth's mom. The woman had been coerced into hacking websites under the threat of someone hurting her daughter. Ty felt certain Alexandria would be cleared. They just needed to give it time. Meanwhile, Annabeth's dad, Joe, remained in a coma after being injected with an unknown substance.

The situation was complicated, to say the least.

Unbelievably, the North Carolina governor had been involved, as well as rogue CIA agents, the head of a pharmaceutical company, and others. It seemed surreal, that was for sure.

Ty prayed that God would protect Cassidy. He couldn't lose her. Not now. Not after all they'd been through.

He cranked his engine and took off down the road.

He needed to check on Annabeth and then gather his guys.

Then they would have a life-changing conversation.

CHAPTER NINE

"WHAT DO you want me to do?" Paige Henderson hurried beside her as Cassidy walked into the station and toward her office.

Cassidy didn't slow down, but she did lower her voice. "There's nothing you can do except listen to whatever the feds ask. They've taken over this investigation and part of this building right now."

"Chief . . ." Alarm filled her voice.

Cassidy paused outside her office and turned toward Paige. "I know it's crazy. But I'm doing everything I can to figure out what's happening here."

"Why would they question you?" Something close to fear quivered in her voice.

"It's complicated. I can't explain it all to you now. Another time, okay?"

Paige stared at her another moment before snapping back into professional mode. "I understand. But, Chief, I don't want to be here with these guys."

"They're not all bad guys."

"But some of them are?" Her voice lilted up in confusion.

Cassidy nibbled on the inside of her lip as she tried to find an answer. Finally, she settled on not saying anything. "Listen, I need to pick up my SUV. Then I have to go to the Blackout headquarters for a bit. Can you hold things down here while I'm gone?"

"Of course." But worry still etched the lines on Paige's forehead.

"Good. Call me if you need anything."

"I will."

With that, Cassidy grabbed an extra set of keys from her desk. She would take one of the cruisers to the crime scene and have another officer drive this vehicle back to the station. She wanted to take her own SUV to the meeting instead of leaving it on the side of the road.

Once inside the vehicle, she texted her officers.

Meet me at the Blackout headquarters at two. We have some important things to discuss.

With that done, she headed down the road. A few minutes later, she pulled up behind her SUV, put the cruiser in Park, then rushed to her own vehicle.

But when she climbed inside, she noticed something on the floor in front of the passenger seat. Something that hadn't been there earlier.

She sucked in a breath as the object came into focus.

It was a chef's knife.

With blood on it.

And it looked just like the ones she and Ty kept at their house.

CASSIDY STARED at the group around her. She hadn't had the chance to organize what she was going to say. But she had no time to waste. A mental time bomb ticked in her ear, reminding her of what was at stake.

She studied the faces of everyone around her. Her three police officers were here: Braden Dillinger, Dane Bradshaw, and Jonathan Banks. The four original members of Blackout were also present: Colton

Locke, Dez Rodriquez, Griff McIntyre, and Benjamin James. Ty and Mac joined her to offer their support.

They'd met in a conference room in the newly dubbed Daniel Oliver Building.

Daniel was a SEAL who'd given his life to save many other lives. The name seemed fitting.

This room was usually used for briefings. All the guys sat at the table while Cassidy stood at the front of the room, trying not to sweat bullets.

Finally, she cleared her throat, knowing she had to start.

"Thank you all for coming. I know a lot has happened over the past few weeks here on Lantern Beach. I feel like I owe you all an explanation—especially since I need your help."

Everybody around her stared, giving her their complete attention. She glanced at Ty, who offered her a nod of encouragement. Then she continued.

"My real name is Cady Matthews, and I was a detective in Seattle for four years." The words felt surreal as they left her lips. "During that time, I was sent on an undercover assignment to infiltrate a gang called DH-7."

"You're Commotio Cordis . . ." Banks stared at her and shook his head, appearing both surprised and maybe even impressed.

She swallowed hard when he mentioned the nickname her underground following had given her. She hadn't heard that name in a long time.

But she would get to that in a minute.

"During my time undercover, I had a confrontation with the gang leader, Raul Sanders," she continued. "In the process, I threw something at him as a last-minute tactic to save myself. The object—a baseball—hit his chest and made his heart stop."

She paused and gave everyone a moment to process what she'd just said. Then her gaze met Banks. "That act earned me the nickname of Commotio Cordis by those in the underground. Afterward, the gang put a bounty on my head, and I became one of the most wanted women in underground America. That's when I came here to Lantern Beach."

"And you changed your name to Cassidy Chambers," Dillinger muttered, slowly nodding with realization.

"Cassidy Livingston at first. I never intended on staying here. And I definitely never intended on falling in love." She cast a soft smile at Ty before turning back to everyone else.

"How could we not have known this?" Bradshaw asked, sounding a bit mystified.

"It was imperative that I keep it quiet. If I told people, not only would I be in danger, but so would anyone who knew. That's why I only told two people here on this island—Ty and Mac. They've helped keep my secret the past few years."

"Why are you telling us now?" Dillinger asked.

"Good question." She drew in a long breath as reality chipped away at any sense of calm. "I was hoping I could put this all behind me and live the rest of my days on the island in peace. But it's become apparent that I cannot. Samuel Stephens was the FBI agent in charge of keeping my identity protected."

"He's the man who died today . . ." Banks clarified.

"Yes," Cassidy said. "I wasn't exactly in witness protection, but I was in something very much like it. There are still people out there who would want to kill me if they knew who I was. There are still people who are that loyal to DH-7."

Bradshaw's discerning gaze met hers. "So why did Samuel Stephens die?"

"That's what I'm trying to figure out. He called me last week and told me he wasn't sure I could trust Special Agent Watkins. Then today, right before he died, he told me 'They know.' And before you ask, I have no idea what that means. I only know that Samuel was stabbed and I was called to a fabricated incident in the woods."

Everyone sat in silence for a moment. It was a lot for anybody to comprehend. And Cassidy understood that.

She only hoped they all understood where she was coming from.

CHAPTER TEN

———

CASSIDY GAVE everyone a couple of minutes to process what she'd said before continuing.

Cassidy sat on a stool at the front of the room, a wave of exhaustion hitting her. She had to push through it. "I didn't like keeping all of you in the dark. I want you all to know that. I only did it because I want to protect people around me."

Bradshaw leaned back in his chair, his arms crossed. "So why *are* you telling us now?"

"The truth is that someone is setting me up to take the fall for this crime. I have to find the person truly responsible before I end up going to jail, or, even worse, before someone gets revenge on me and hands my head over to DH-7."

"What can we do?" Colton straightened in his seat, looking like a soldier waiting for instructions.

"I'm asking that you be vigilant. Keep your eyes open for any signs of trouble. But mostly, I just want you all to trust me. I know that's hard since I was keeping secrets. But you've got to know that I would have never killed Samuel. He was one of the few people I trusted, and I owed my life to him."

Bradshaw's body language relaxed slightly as he leaned forward and against the table. "Do you have any idea who could be setting you up?"

"I've been trying to think it through, and I've narrowed it down to a few suspects. If you'll bear with me, I'll tell you who they are."

"Please do," Griff said.

Cassidy drew in a deep breath. As she shifted on the stool, Ty handed her a bottle of water. She took a sip before continuing.

"My first suspect is Special Agent Watkins," Cassidy said. "Samuel never told me why he didn't trust the man. Part of me wonders if he was coming to the island to tell me those reasons. I guess I'll never know that for sure, though.

"A second person is Governor Hollick. He's hiding secrets, and he'll do anything to protect them. He doesn't care who gets in his way, even if it's someone who saved his life on more than one occasion."

Colton leaned forward in his seat. "You really think the governor would do something like this?"

Cassidy shrugged and took another sip of her water. "I'm not pointing fingers. But his name has popped up recently, more than once, and I believe he's corrupt."

"Who else?" Banks asked.

"This one might sound the most outrageous, but I'm going to share it anyway." Cassidy swallowed hard. "You remember the two former CIA agents who were arrested on the island last week, Lars and Emma Shackleford?"

A knot formed on Banks' forehead. "They're in jail, right?"

"Yes, they are. But they claimed a man named Gerald Mecklenburg framed them for the murder of one of their CIA colleagues."

"That's why Lars and Emma went rogue," Bradshaw said.

"Exactly," Cassidy said. "That's supposedly why they blackmailed so many people. They wanted to take their former boss down. I've been doing some research on this Mecklenburg guy in my spare time, and he's done some questionable things. Then again, he's CIA, so it's halfway expected. But he could have something to do with this."

"But the Shacklefords were criminals." Dillinger shrugged, clearly skeptical. "Who's to say they were telling the truth?"

"Exactly. Maybe they weren't. For that matter, we don't know the truth right now. Which leads me to my last suspects." Cassidy drew in a deep breath. "Members of DH-7."

She pressed a button on the remote in her hand and pictures of various gang members appeared on the screen behind her. Ty had put these together for her before she arrived.

"This is what they looked like last time I saw them," she continued. "But they're smarter than you might think. Especially the leaders. They're very cunning. I wouldn't put it past them to change their appearance in order to blend in. As far as I know, these three are still some of the remaining leaders of DH-7. Others have already been arrested."

"Do you want us to see if they're on the island?" Banks scratched his head, as if trying to figure out their next step.

"I'd definitely love for you to keep your eyes open for them. I also need to find out when and how Samuel Stephens arrived on the island and where he was staying. The FBI will be watching us, so we have to watch our steps. It's best if the FBI doesn't think any of you are aligned with me right now."

"I certainly don't want them to think that I'm aligned with them." Dillinger frowned as he crossed his arms.

Cassidy appreciated his words. She really did. But she didn't want anyone to get in trouble because of her.

"Just be careful," she finally said. "I won't be able to forgive myself if one of you takes the fall for something I did."

Bradshaw rose to his feet. "I'll stand behind you."

Banks also rose. "Me too."

Dillinger stood as well. "Me three."

Gratitude filled her, and a smile of relief stretched across her face. "Thank you, guys. You have no idea how much this means to me."

"I think I can speak for the whole team here at Blackout when I say we have your back," Colton said. "We'd be more than happy to offer whatever you need, including extra security. It sounds like you're going to need it."

Another wave of relief washed through her. "I am going to need it. More than I ever imagined."

TY WATCHED as Cassidy stood at the front of the room telling everybody secrets that were never supposed to be muttered aloud.

He never thought the day would come when he'd see this.

But he felt like a weight had been lifted off his chest now that he didn't have to keep the truth to himself. He hadn't realized how burdened it had made him feel.

Cassidy had been so composed the entire time she spoke, even though Ty knew this couldn't be easy on her.

After she finished, several guys lingered to talk. But Cassidy had to usher her officers back to work, knowing it would be suspicious if they stayed here too long. The feds would start asking questions.

Eventually, only Cassidy, Mac, and Ty were left.

Cassidy's face turned even more serious as she looked at them, and Ty sensed that she had something she needed to say.

She reached into her bag and pulled something out. His eyes widened when he saw an evidence bag with a bloody knife inside—a knife that matched the ones from their house.

"This was in my SUV when I climbed back inside," she told them.

"Is that . . . ?" Mac stared at it as if he didn't want to believe what he was seeing.

Cassidy frowned. "I'm nearly certain this is the knife used to kill Samuel."

Ty felt his lungs freeze. "Someone planted it in your SUV? How? Was your door unlocked?"

"My guess is that they picked the lock. Whoever is behind this is smart. They know what they're doing."

"I'd say so . . ." Mac muttered.

"They're setting me up for this. I don't know why. I don't know who. But someone is behind this, and they're determined to make me take the fall."

"I agree," Mac said. "That's the only reason this person wouldn't try to kill you while you were out in those woods. He had another plan all along."

Ty's gut knotted. He didn't like the sound of those words.

"I don't know what to do with it," Cassidy said. "As an officer of the law, I *should* turn it in. I know I should. But I also know if I turn it in, I'll be arrested. I have no doubt my prints are on this. I dusted it for prints, and I'll send them off to the lab, just to be certain no other prints are there. I marked the file as a break in, hoping it won't raise any suspicions."

"Probably a good idea," Mac said.

Cassidy's gaze met his a moment and she nodded before she focused on her husband.

"It's just one of our ordinary knives." Ty shrugged. "It's anybody's guess when it went missing. And did someone break in just to steal it? Or did someone we invited into our house take it?"

The question made Cassidy's breath catch. "I don't even want to think that it could be someone we know and trust."

"We shouldn't take anyone off the table," Mac said.

"You're right. We shouldn't."

"Who have you had over recently?" Mac continued.

"We've had the Bible study group over," Ty started. "Social workers. Police. The Blackout guys."

"Anyone out of the ordinary?"

Ty and Cassidy exchanged a look.

"We did have someone over to check our cable box," Cassidy said. "Our TV stopped working, so the company sent a tech over from the mainland."

Mac straightened. "When was that?"

"Four days ago," Ty said. "That has to be it. I left

him alone for probably five minutes so I could fix the dresser drawer in Annabeth's room. It came off the track. I can call the cable company and see what they say, but he's the one person who makes sense."

"I agree." Cassidy let out a long, burdened sigh. "So now I need to figure out what to do. What the right thing is. Because if Watkins finds this in my possession . . ."

"Or if they realize that you've been hiding it . . ." Mac raised his eyebrows.

Cassidy frowned again. "Exactly. I'm a sitting duck."

"We need to think this through before we make any decisions," Ty said. "In the meantime, we need to put it somewhere where the feds won't find it."

"But where?" Cassidy asked. "If I bring it back to our house and they find it, I'll clearly look guilty. But if I leave it anywhere else, then somebody else might look guilty by association."

"Give it to me." Ty reached out his hand. "I'll figure out what to do with it."

"Are you sure?" Cassidy stared at him uncertainly, a war being fought in her gaze.

"I'm positive. I'm not going to tell you where I put it. But it will be somewhere no one will find it."

"Don't tell me where you put it either," Mac said. "I'm going to try to forget this conversation."

"And that brings me to my last question," Cassidy said. "If someone planted this evidence, then what else did they plant?"

Her question hung in the air.

CHAPTER ELEVEN

TY TRIED to shrug off the anger and frustration building inside him. Somebody was framing his wife. Someone powerful, most likely. And if Ty and Cassidy weren't careful, this person might get away with it.

How could he brush off something like that?

He couldn't.

He moved through the woods outside the Blackout facility, the bloody knife in his pocket.

Guilt haunted him with every step. But his hand had been forced. He couldn't let his wife take the fall for something she didn't do.

Yet he knew what he was doing wasn't necessarily the right thing either. The lines were blurred.

As he continued through the trees, memories flooded him.

Two years ago, a cult had set up camp on these very grounds. The cult leader, a man named Anthony Gilead, had discovered an old World War II bunker hidden on this island not far from the Blackout complex. He'd managed to grab Ty and chain him inside.

Ty had been through a lot of things as a Navy SEAL. But that experience ranked right up there with the worst of them.

If it hadn't been for Cassidy, he might have died down there.

That was the thing about their relationship he cherished most. He and Cassidy fought for each other. They looked out for each other. And they understood each other.

That's why Ty knew he would do whatever it took to help her now.

He reached the entrance of the bunker. The heavy metal doors leading into it had become covered with vines in the short period since it had been abandoned. Anyone passing by wouldn't notice the passage leading underground.

But Ty would never forget where it was.

He reached down and opened one of the doors.

The dank scent of earth and mold drifted up to him, along with a burst of cooler air.

His chest tightened as he stepped inside the dark space.

Memories tried to attack him, to make his mind a prison of its own as Ty relived those moments when death had taunted him.

But he couldn't let that happen.

When he reached the bottom of the steps, he placed the knife in a corner, careful to wipe away any fingerprints on the evidence bag. If the police ever found this, Ty definitely didn't want his prints or Cassidy's to be found on it.

Not that he thought the police would find this.

But he had to be careful.

He found a loose stone and placed it over the knife.

With a glance back, he took the stairs two at a time as he headed outside. He slammed the door shut and pulled the vines back over the entrance. Then Ty picked up a few dried leaves left over from winter and threw them on top as well, doing everything he could to conceal the space.

He stared at the doors one more moment, noticing how they blended in with nature.

Cassidy should be safe.

For now, at least.

But he had no idea what else might be in store.

CASSIDY NEEDED to get back to the station, but there was one thing she needed to do first.

At the Blackout building, she climbed the steps to the second floor and headed down the hall. This was the residential area where the full-time staff had oversized apartments.

It was still hard for her to believe how this area had been transformed.

Just two years ago, these grounds had been a place of nightmares. But now, the old buildings had been cleared and these new buildings had been financed and built.

In some ways, they reminded her of her life.

So much of what had defined her had been erased, and there was a new person living in place of the old one. Yet the basics were still the same.

But all that was on the line right now.

Her stomach clenched at the thought of it.

Cassidy paused by one of the apartments and knocked. A moment later, Bethany McIntyre opened the door and grinned at her. The pretty blonde was married to Griff.

"Cassidy!" Her cheerful voice was a welcome relief in the midst of bad news. "Good to see you."

"I have a few minutes, so I just wanted to stop by and see Annabeth. I hope that's okay."

"Of course. Come on inside. The girls are playing with some Barbie dolls.

Cassidy followed Bethany through the apartment into the bedroom where her four-year-old daughter, Ada, stayed. As she did, Samuel's last words replayed in her mind.

They know.

What had he meant by that?

Who was he talking about?

If Cassidy knew those answers, she might be able to find his killer.

She put the thought aside and paused in the doorway, watching the girls play for a moment. Six-year-old Annabeth had dark hair that reached her shoulders. Her dark eyes were intelligent. Her figure was thin and petite.

A smile broadened Cassidy's lips as Annabeth brushed her Barbie's hair and picked out a new princess outfit for her to wear.

She'd enjoyed having Annabeth at her house.

But, in her heart, she felt like their time together was coming to an end soon.

Not that Cassidy didn't want Annabeth to stay with her forever. If it came down to it, Cassidy would welcome the girl with open arms for as long as forever. But Annabeth deserved to be with her parents, and her parents deserved to be with her. Cassidy would never stand in the way of that.

The sight of the girl made her heart twinge bittersweetly.

Annabeth saw Cassidy and sprang from the floor. She rushed toward Cassidy and threw her arms around her.

The girl had what was called traumatic mutism, but she'd been making strides lately. Still, the girl didn't have any type of conversations other than nonverbal.

"It looks like you're having fun," Cassidy said.

Annabeth nodded and grinned. The next instant, she darted back to Ada to continue playing.

"Aren't they cute?" Bethany smiled down at the girls.

"They're adorable." Cassidy glanced at her friend. "How are you feeling?"

Bethany and another friend, Elise, had recently announced that they were both pregnant. Cassidy was thrilled for her friends. But their celebratory news felt sometimes like a stab in the heart to her.

She'd been longing to make that same announcement.

But the doctor had told her that wouldn't be possible—at least not on her own. She and Ty had considered IVF but ultimately decided that this wasn't the best time. It would require too many visits off the island and would put Cassidy too much at risk.

And now, after everything that happened today . . . it seemed like an even worse idea.

If Cassidy didn't give every effort to finding Samuel's killer, she might end up in jail for a crime she didn't commit. All her visions of having a happy family could disappear forever.

Tension gripped her chest at the thought until she felt like she could hardly breathe.

"Cassidy?"

Cassidy looked up and realized that Bethany had said something. "I'm sorry, what was that?"

"You seem distracted today. Is everything okay?"

Cassidy didn't want her friends to worry so she brushed the observation off with the wave of her hand. "It's okay. I just have a lot on my mind."

"That's understandable." Bethany patted her back. "Just let me know what I can do."

"You're doing so much right now helping out with Annabeth. Ty and I really appreciate this."

"Oh, it's no problem. Just let me know what you need, and I'm there for you."

Cassidy wished for a moment that she could tell her friend everything that was going on. But not now. She was still exhausted from sharing what she had with the group earlier. Vulnerability was refreshing—but also fatiguing.

Cassidy took a step back. "I've got to get back to work, but call me if I can do anything."

"Of course," Bethany said. "You take care of yourself, Cassidy."

Cassidy told Annabeth goodbye and then left.

But taking care of herself seemed like an impossible task considering the circumstances.

CHAPTER TWELVE

AS CASSIDY LEFT the Blackout headquarters and pulled through the gates leading from the complex, she glanced around.

Why did she feel like she was being watched? It didn't make sense. All that surrounded her here were woods and marshes. Not that someone couldn't be between those trees or between the reeds. But she saw no one.

Maybe she was just paranoid. Maybe everything that had happened had chipped away at her reasoning.

Either way, she couldn't let emotions get the best of her. She needed to remain sharp if she was going to get through this.

And for Ty's sake, she had to get through this.

It was clear that somebody didn't want to kill her right now. They simply wanted to implicate her. To make her pay.

The one thing she wasn't sure about was why.

She gripped her steering wheel as she continued down the road.

It would be easy to blame this on DH-7. But what was happening appeared more complicated than what those gang members seemed capable of. These crimes didn't echo the offenses they'd committed in the past. Instead, this new turn of events seemed to have been executed by someone with more sophistication, power, and money.

But the question was who. All the suspects she'd mentioned earlier still swirled in her mind.

Right now, she was going to go back to the office and try to sort through them all.

Yes, back to the office.

She couldn't let Watkins and his men intimidate her. That was her space, and she was going to use it. She'd let them take over the conference room, but that was it.

And she was going to keep her chin up. If there was one thing her parents had taught her, it was to show strength even in weakness. Her father was one of the wealthiest men in the United States, but the treasures he'd had in front of him had gone ignored. Namely, Cassidy and her mother. Their relationship had always been strained, and when Cassidy had gone into hiding, it became mostly nonexistent.

Funny how she thought about them now as everything was on the line. You never forgot your roots, she supposed.

Cassidy pulled up to the station and climbed out of her SUV. She stared at the front door a brief moment, drawing in a deep breath.

As she stepped inside, she knew she had to put on the show of her life.

TY GOT BACK to the Blackout headquarters, still unable to shake what he'd just done.

But dwelling on it would do him no good. Regret would only cripple him right now—and that wasn't acceptable.

Instead, he went straight to his office, sat down behind his desk, and pulled out his phone.

One of his former Navy SEAL colleagues now worked for the FBI. As far as Ty knew, Harry Overton had probably only been at the bureau for about six months so he was still a rookie. But the man had always been sharp. He and Ty had had each other's backs on more than one mission.

Ty hoped that his friend might have his back now as well.

After only a brief second of hesitation, he dialed Harry's number and listened to the rings on the other end.

Five seconds in, his friend answered. "Special Agent Harry Overton."

"Harry," Ty started. "It's Chambers."

"There's a name I haven't heard in a while. How are you doing, man?"

"I'm hanging in," Ty said. "I wish I was calling just to catch up and see how you're doing."

"I understand. What's going on?"

Ty's gaze fell on a picture he had on his desk of him and Cassidy. A bittersweet smile tugged at his lips as he remembered being on the beach with her that evening at sunset. He would fight for this woman until the very end. The two of them needed more sunset pictures together. They'd vowed to take a new one each year—all the way until they were gray and wrinkled.

"We have an interesting situation going on here in Lantern Beach," Ty started. "It involves an FBI agent. Someone named Donald Watkins. You ever heard of the guy before?"

"What field office is he based out of?"

"Raleigh."

"I can't say I've heard of him. What's going on with him?"

Ty sucked in a breath before continuing. "Someone hinted that he's dirty. The man is working with my wife, who's the police chief here at Lantern Beach. I'm worried about her."

Harry paused before asking, "So you want me to see what I can find out?"

"I don't want to put you or your job at risk. But I wondered if you might just ask around."

"For you? I'll see what I can do. And I'll try to do it quickly, as it sounds like the situation is timely."

"It is. I really appreciate any help you might be able to offer me on this."

"That's no problem. I'll be in touch."

Ty leaned back and let out a breath. At least there was that.

But it wouldn't be enough. Ty needed to do whatever he could to get to the bottom of the situation.

That meant he was going to head to all the rental office locations this morning. He wanted to check the security footage of anybody who'd checked into vacation homes over the past week.

Doing so would take a long time. In fact, maybe he'd get one of his Blackout guys to help him.

But the best way to see who was on this island was to look at that footage.

Ty had no time to waste. He needed to get busy.

CHAPTER THIRTEEN

CASSIDY MADE it into her office without running into Watkins. Once inside, she closed the door, locked it, and told Paige to get her only if it was an emergency.

Cassidy had too many other things on her mind right now, and she needed some time alone. Time when she wasn't being watched.

Everybody thought she was tough, and Cassidy knew in most ways she *was* tough.

But even tough people had their limitations. Had their moments of weakness. And Cassidy felt like she was on the verge of losing it right now. Like if she allowed herself, tears might flow freely down her cheeks.

She wasn't ready for that.

But she did need a moment to breathe and gather her thoughts.

Her mind raced over everything that happened until stopping on two thoughts.

First, she needed to figure out who Samuel's supervisor was.

She made several phone calls, trying to keep her identity quiet as she asked questions. But thirty minutes later she was left with the conclusion that Samuel didn't have anyone over him.

It sounded strange. But it appeared Samuel worked on his own, doing various jobs with the FBI as needed. Certainly, he answered to someone. But Cassidy was at a loss as to how to find out who that was.

Her search had gotten her nowhere.

But she had one other question she wanted to explore. It had to do with Alexandria Manchester.

The woman had been taken captive by the Shacklefords, who were now in jail and had pleaded the fifth. The Shacklefords had attempted to send a text revealing Cassidy's identity to the world, but Mac had jammed their cell phone before it happened. Alexandria had also wiped the couple's computer before the FBI grabbed it.

But Cassidy had to wonder exactly what Alexandria might know—and if anyone wanted to use that information as leverage for a bigger purpose.

The woman *could* have some information that would help break this case open. After all, Samuel must have discovered *something* that made him think Watkins couldn't be trusted. Did Alexandria know that secret also?

Cassidy picked up the phone and called the jail where Alexandria was being held until her trial.

A deputy answered, and Cassidy explained who she was before asking if she might speak with Alexandria.

The man put her on hold before coming back a few minutes later. "I'm sorry, Chief Chambers. There's no Alexandria Manchester registered here."

Cassidy's back stiffened as she mentally replayed his words. "It's my understanding that she's being held at your facility. Has she been recently transferred?"

"From what I can tell, she was never here."

It just didn't make any sense. Where in the world could the woman be?

The only person Cassidy could think of who might know that answer was Special Agent Watkins. She had a feeling he wouldn't be quick to share anything with her.

"Is there any other way I can find out where she's being held right now?" Cassidy asked the deputy. "It's important for a case we're working on."

"I would talk with her arresting officer. He or she is the best place to start."

Great. That left Cassidy talking to Watkins again. That would be a dead end. There had to be another way she could find out.

Cassidy ended the call and leaned back, that feeling of impending doom continuing to churn in her stomach.

AFTER SEVERAL MINUTES OF CONTEMPLATION, Cassidy stood from her desk.

She wasn't going to be a doormat.

With hardened resolve, she opened the door to her office and stormed down the hallway toward the conference room.

Watkins looked up as she stepped inside. He'd been seated at the table with three other agents. Papers were spread everywhere. Pictures had been tacked to a board in the corner.

He stood. "Chief Chambers. Can I help you?"

"Where are you holding Alexandria Manchester?"

His gaze flickered. "Why do you want to know?"

"That's not important. Where is she?"

His narrowed gaze turned into a glare. "Do I need to remind you, Chief, that it isn't your case? I told you to stay out of my investigation, and you didn't. Obviously, I should have arrested you right then. If I had, then maybe we wouldn't be down another FBI agent."

His words had been meant to feel like a slap in the face—and it had worked. A flash of Samuel's last moments filled Cassidy's mind. Then her resolve strengthened even more.

She had to figure out who was responsible for her friend's death.

She leveled her gaze. "I didn't hurt Samuel, and you're not going to intimidate me. Now, where is Alexandria?"

"That information is on a need-to-know basis."

Cassidy felt more anger simmering inside her. She understood that this man didn't trust her. Maybe he was even dirty. But he wasn't playing fair right now.

"Do you need to be reminded that I am the guardian of this woman's child? I'd say that I should be on that need-to-know list—not as an officer of the law but as someone who's taking care of the woman's child."

Watkins tilted his head, an annoyed expression on his face. "I understand that. But I'm not sure I can tell you any information concerning my case. Too much about it is classified—and out of your league."

"You mean jurisdiction?"

His look made it clear he'd used the correct word the first time.

Cassidy shook her head. "I deserve to know more. If you don't offer me information pertaining to the child in my care, then I'll find it out myself."

He stepped closer. Everyone else in the room had gone quiet and watched them.

"I don't think that you're in any position to give me ultimatums," Watkins growled.

Cassidy held her ground, knowing better than to show any sign of weakness. "This isn't an ultimatum. It's a statement of intent."

Watkins stared at her another moment before shaking his head.

Before he had a chance to offer any type of come-back, Cassidy turned and left.

But she'd seen one other thing in that room, something that had given her insight on this case.

Pictures and information had been posted on the wall behind the conference table—one that appeared to let the FBI try to organize their thoughts as well as the evidence.

Under the word "Suspects" was a picture of Cassidy.

CHAPTER FOURTEEN

AN HOUR LATER, Cassidy paused as she stepped into The Crazy Chefette.

She needed to grab something to eat—it was already past dinnertime. But the real reason she'd come was because Bradshaw had asked if they could meet. She figured it was better if they didn't speak at the station, especially since so many feds were around.

As the scent of fresh crab cakes and Old Bay filled her, she glanced around. Funny how the aromas could make her feel a strange measure of comfort, even in the midst of this turmoil.

She spotted Bradshaw at the corner table. She slid into the booth across from him and ordered a water and hamburger with fries. It wasn't her normal meal choice, but today the comfort food sounded too tempting to resist.

"What's going on?" she asked, anxious to know if he had an update for her.

Bradshaw scooted his plate out of the way. He'd already gotten his food and had eaten most of it.

"I spent the afternoon talking to people here on the island." He leaned closer. "I discovered that Samuel checked into the inn last night."

Cassidy held her breath, wondering where he would go with this. "And?"

"The innkeeper said that he didn't arrive until about eleven. He didn't have much to say, and he left early this morning."

"Did he just book one night?"

"He booked three. But he asked if there was a possibility of more if needed. The innkeeper told him that there was, that this wasn't their busy season yet."

"What about his personal belongings? Are they still there?"

Bradshaw frowned and shook his head. "The feds already figured out where he was staying. They came about an hour before I got there and collected everything. But according to the innkeeper, Stephens only brought one bag."

Cassidy let that information sink into her thoughts. "When did he book?"

"He booked about five hours before he arrived. It was pretty last minute."

Cassidy paused as her food was delivered. She thanked the waitress and waited until she was gone before speaking again. "It almost sounds like Samuel discovered something and wanted to tell me face-to-face rather than over the phone."

"Why couldn't he say something over the phone?"

"The only thing I can think of is that he wondered if his phone might have been bugged." She picked up a fry and nibbled on it as she let her thoughts turn over in her mind.

"Do you think someone would have gone that far?"

Cassidy didn't have to think about her answer before nodding. "Depending on what's going on here, I know they would."

He leaned even closer and lowered his voice. "I haven't been at the police station all day. None of us have. Have you checked your office recently to see if there's anything there?"

Bradshaw's words made a lot of sense. The feds weren't playing fair here. One of their own had died, and they would do anything to find the person responsible. Maybe Cassidy would do the same thing if she were in their shoes.

"I haven't checked my office for bugs in the past day or so," Cassidy said. "I just checked the space last week. But you're right, I should check again. I'll have Ty come in and do that for me."

"Good idea." Bradshaw straightened before shaking his head. "Listen, Chief. I don't like any of this."

"And I'm sorry I put you all in this position." She truly was. If she could turn back time, she realized that maybe leaving Lantern Beach after she faked her death would have been the best choice. Not getting attached. Keeping people at arm's length. But the relationships she'd built were invaluable.

His gaze locked on hers. "Don't apologize. We need to have each other's backs. I just feel like there are greater powers at play here."

"You're afraid these greater powers are going to be the ultimate victors?" Cassidy tried to read between the lines of what he was saying.

"No way," Bradshaw said. "I just know we have a tough fight ahead of us. Let me know what I can do for you. In the meantime, I'm going to keep my eyes open for anyone who might resemble a member of DH-7."

Cassidy nodded. "Thank you."

A moment later, Bradshaw slipped out of the booth and left Cassidy to eat.

AS SOON AS BRADSHAW LEFT, Cassidy's friend Lisa slid into the booth in his place. She owned this restaurant and was the mother of an adorable baby girl named Julia. Cassidy was so happy for her friend —for all her friends who'd started this next chapter of their lives. But grief still filled her when she thought about the fact that her dreams might not ever come to fruition.

Then again, maybe it was better that way. That's what she kept telling herself, at least. Cassidy was in no position to bring a child into the world—not with all the ghosts that haunted her.

"There's something weird in the air on this island," Lisa whispered. "Can you feel it too?"

Great. Her friend, as a civilian, was sensing something also.

Out of all the people here on the island, Lisa was probably Cassidy's closest friend. Her husband was

Braden Dillinger, one of Cassidy's officers. Although everyone had promised to keep Cassidy's secret, she knew it would be hard for Dillinger to keep this news from his wife.

Cassidy needed to tell her. She wanted Lisa to hear this from her. But this wasn't the time or the place.

"I'm sure you heard about the FBI agent who was found in the woods," Cassidy started.

Lisa leaned closer. "Another FBI agent came in here earlier today. He was asking about you."

Cassidy bristled but tried to keep her composure. "What did you tell him?"

"I told him that you were in here for breakfast this morning and that you stayed for about an hour before going into work. Did I say something wrong?"

"Not at all," Cassidy said. "You should tell the truth. For sure."

Lisa shook her head, not bothering to hide how perplexed she felt. "I just don't understand . . ."

Cassidy dropped the fry back onto the plate and leaned across the table. "Listen, there's a lot going on here. There are things that I need to tell you. But I can't do it here. And I can't do it now. I just know that you and I need to talk. I want you to hear the truth from me."

Her friend's eyes widened. "You're scaring me, Cassidy."

"There's no need to be scared of the truth. But there are things I haven't been able to say because I wanted to keep people safe. Just know that I consider you a good friend, and that I'll tell you everything. But, right now, I need to concentrate on clearing my name. The FBI thinks I had something to do with that agent's death."

Lisa gasped. "What?"

"They're looking for someone to blame, and I was the one out there in the woods with him. Plus, I'd talked to this agent a couple of times before that. So now they think I might have been involved somehow."

"I guess the good news is that they haven't arrested you."

Cassidy's spine tightened. "No, they haven't. Not yet."

But Cassidy didn't know how long that would remain true.

They know.

Samuel's last words again replayed in her mind.

They would haunt her until she had answers.

CHAPTER FIFTEEN

AS CASSIDY STEPPED from The Crazy Chefette, a brunette in a business suit practically pounced on her.

"I'm Tina Andrews with *US News Today*," the woman rushed. "I'm here to cover the story of the FBI agent who was killed in the line of duty. Police Chief Chambers, can you give me a quote?"

As a camera flashed, panic surged through her. Cassidy shielded her face, knowing being photographed was too risky.

Instead, Cassidy kept her head down and kept walking.

She'd known reporters would show up sooner or later. She just hadn't expected them to track her down.

"No comment," she muttered, desperate to get away.

"Is it true the FBI has a suspect they're zeroing in on?"

Cassidy's lungs nearly froze at Tina's words. *Cassidy* was their suspect. How long until reporters learned that information?

She kept walking, even as the woman hurried along beside her, her heels clicking on the sidewalk.

"No comment," she told the woman again.

"What *can* you tell me?"

Cassidy climbed inside her SUV and slammed the door.

As she started the engine, she saw that the woman was nearly pressed against her window, not taking no for an answer. Cassidy could back out and pray the woman moved out of the way.

But the driven look in the reporter's eyes made Cassidy think that might not happen.

Finally, she cracked her window just enough to talk—but not enough to be photographed. "The FBI is in charge of this investigation. You'll need to talk to Special Agent Watkins. That's all I can say."

"What role is the Lantern Beach Police Department taking in this investigation?"

But Cassidy was done with this conversation.

She put her SUV into Reverse and started to slowly back up.

Finally, the woman stepped away.

Cassidy pulled from the restaurant, her heart still pounding.

That reporter had ambushed her. There were probably more journalists out there just like her. It wouldn't take long before they showed up here.

Just as before, the invisible time bomb kept ticking in her head, promising an explosion soon if she wasn't careful.

* * *

TY RAN his scanner around Cassidy's office.

So far, he hadn't found anything. But the fact that Cassidy had asked him to do this sent up red flags. She thought the feds had bugged her office, didn't she?

He frowned. He wouldn't put it past them.

The last place he checked was Cassidy's desk. As he ran the wand beneath the top, his device beeped.

Ty reached in and felt around the smooth edges of the wood—until his fingers hit something hard. He grabbed it and pulled out a half-inch device.

A bug.

He sucked in a breath as he examined it.

He'd just checked Cassidy's office last week—which meant someone had put this here recently.

If he had to guess, the FBI had gotten a warrant to plant this, especially considering they thought Cassidy was a suspect. As soon as they had anything more than circumstantial evidence, these guys would probably arrest her.

They'd take Cassidy into custody.

Ty couldn't let that happen.

He dropped the bug on the floor and crushed it beneath his shoe. Hopefully, Cassidy hadn't said anything compromising while in her office. Ty knew she was careful.

But he'd need to ask her and make sure.

Ty checked the rest of the desk to be certain nothing had been missed.

No other listening devices were there.

Just as he cleaned up the remains of the bug and placed it in a plastic bag, the door opened. Cassidy stepped inside, questions in her gaze.

Her eyes immediately went to the bag in his hands. Then she mouthed, "You found something?"

"The rest of the place is clear." He pushed the door closed behind her. "But I found a bug underneath your desk. I took care of it."

She let her head fall back against the door as she pressed her eyes closed. "This keeps getting worse."

"I know. But we're working on it. Have you been careful about what you've said when you've been here?"

"Of course. All my meetings have been offsite."

"That's what I figured. You might want to keep it that way. I'll check your purse too and anywhere else somebody could have dropped something."

She let out a sigh and shook her head before squeezing the skin between her eyes. "What a nightmare."

He pulled Cassidy into his arms, sensing how overwhelmed she was right now. Ty hadn't seen her like this in a long time. The reaction never came when she was worried about herself—only when she was worried about people she cared about.

"We'll get through this," he murmured.

"How can you be so sure?"

"Because you're Cassidy Chambers. We've weathered a lot of storms since we've been together. We'll weather this one too."

She glanced up, her eyes full of doubts. "Ty, if they arrest me—"

"Let's not talk about that." He shushed her.

"But it's important. What if—"

Ty shook his head as his heart crashed into his chest. "We're not going to let it get that far."

A frown tugged at her lips. Her gaze clearly showed she wanted to believe his words. But on a logical level, she was struggling to do so.

"We're not any closer to finding any answers," she finally said. "Unless you saw something when you went to the rental agency offices."

He sighed, wishing he had better news. "I looked through the videos there. I even had Colton help me. But we didn't find anything. I knew it was a long shot."

Cassidy nodded, not looking surprised. "These guys . . . if they're here . . . they probably went through a private rental. There are less ways for them to be found out that way."

Ty leaned back against her desk as he tried to think everything through. "Is there a way you could get a subpoena so you could check those records?"

"Not if this is the FBI's case and if I'm their main suspect."

"Good point." Ty sighed. "What now?"

Cassidy glanced at her watch. "It's getting dark outside. As much as I want to stay here and keep working, I'm exhausted. I don't think there's anything else I can do right now."

"Then maybe we should head to the Blackout campus. I think it's a good idea if we stay there tonight and get a good night's rest. That way we can start fresh in the morning. I'll be there to help you."

She slowly nodded. "That sounds good. Thank you, Ty."

He pulled her toward him and kissed her forehead. "Anytime, my love. Anytime."

CHAPTER SIXTEEN

CASSIDY AND TY snacked on popcorn and brownies while playing UNO with Annabeth before eating a late dinner together. After watching a cartoon on TV, they then tucked the girl into bed.

The moment seemed so normal—even though nothing was normal. Still, Cassidy reveled in the simplicity of it all. She relished the clean scent of Annabeth's hair as the girl had hugged her good night. She treasured the feel of Annabeth's arms around her.

Cassidy knew these times would be coming to an end soon.

A few minutes after Annabeth had been tucked in with her favorite teddy bear, a knock sounded at their apartment. They'd decided to stay on the

Blackout campus until this passed. Being here offered an extra layer of security—security they desperately needed right now.

All the Blackout guys had apartments here.

Normally, Kujo would bark to alert them if someone was at the door, but Ty had let the dog outside to wander the grounds.

Ty strode toward the door, the tension across his shoulders obvious. He halfway expected trouble, didn't he? However, this campus was secure, so the only people within the fence were those with Blackout.

As Ty opened the door, a man Cassidy had never seen before stood on the other side.

He was tall, at least six feet if not more, with blond hair and a neat matching beard.

As soon as Ty saw him, his shoulders relaxed, and he pulled the man into a hug.

"If it isn't Rocco Foster . . ." Ty muttered. "You're here already."

"Just got into town." A British accent flowed through the man's words. "I wanted to stop by and say hi."

Ty turned toward Cassidy. "I'd like for you to meet my wife, Cassidy. Cassidy this is Rocco—not to be confused with the island lawyer, Ricco. *Rocco* is one of our new recruits."

"Nice to meet you." Cassidy always enjoyed meeting Ty's friends, but she had to admit that today wasn't the best time for it. Still, she leaned against the back of the couch, watching the reunion take place.

"Rocco is a former SEAL." Ty ushered his friend inside and shut the door.

"A SEAL or the British equivalent of a SEAL?" The accent had thrown Cassidy for a loop. Weren't all SEALs American?

"My dad is American and my mom British," Rocco explained. "We split our time between the two countries, and I have dual citizenship. I was very blessed to be able to eventually make it as a SEAL."

"The good thing about this guy is that he is just as smart when it comes to all things tactical as he is at being a great diplomat," Ty said. "It's a mix that not many people can master."

Cassidy could tell by the way the man dressed and looked that he was someone who took good care of himself. Most of the SEALs here liked to wear cargo pants and black T-shirts. But this man wore gray dress slacks and a white button-up shirt. His beard was neat, and overall he looked well-groomed, more like a businessman than a tactical operative.

"Are the rest of the guys here?" Ty asked.

"Not yet. But they'll be coming soon. Colton asked me to arrive early so I could get a feel for the place."

"I can't wait for you to meet the rest of the team," Ty told Cassidy. "No Smile Beckett is someone you don't easily forget."

"No Smile Beckett?" Cassidy repeated, curious about the nickname.

"It's nearly impossible to get a grin out of that guy," Ty explained. "Then we also have Homeboy Axle. He actually grew up here on Lantern Beach before joining the military. When he left, he didn't look back. But somehow, Rocco convinced him to join up with the team."

"I guess that goes back to that diplomacy that I'm supposedly so good at." Rocco winked before shrugging in a self-deprecating way.

"And then there's Enough Said Junior."

"Again, an interesting nickname," Cassidy muttered.

"That's because he's the youngest member of the team," Rocco explained. "He actually injured a shoulder while on assignment as a SEAL and had to leave the force. We like to get under his skin by calling him Junior. It's not nice, but he's easy to pick on."

"It sounds like quite the gang that will be joining here." Cassidy had always loved the comradery between the guys. When you had to trust others with your life, it wasn't an option to work as individuals. They had to be a team in order to survive.

"Listen, I don't want to hold you up." Rocco nodded toward the door. "I'd love to catch up sometime. But I know you're probably anxious to get some rest right now."

"I'd love to catch up sometime soon also," Ty said. "I'm assuming that Colton is showing you around? Or is he just letting you fend for yourself?"

"He's going to meet me downstairs in a moment. First, he stopped next door to check on his lovely wife. He'll be down soon."

"I'll give you a call tomorrow, and we'll set something up."

After a couple more minutes of conversation, they said good night, and Ty closed the door.

"Seems like a fun group." Cassidy stood from where she leaned against the couch.

"They are a fun group. I think you're really going to like them all."

"Blackout's really growing. I'm truly impressed, honey. You guys are bringing in more revenue, and you've even been able to make more hires. Not just agents either. But you've been able to get a full-time maintenance guy and cook. Who would have thought all this would have been possible even just two years ago?"

Ty's hands went to his hips, and a contented smile passed his lips. "We have been blessed, that's for sure."

Cassidy knew he was anxious to catch up with his friend. And she was anxious to get to sleep. "Listen, I'm going to turn in a little early tonight. Why don't you go and talk to your friends? I'm okay being by myself."

"Are you sure?" Doubt tinged his voice.

"I'm positive." She reached up on her tiptoes and kissed Ty's cheek. Some time with friends could be just what the doctor ordered for Ty. It would be good for his soul. "I'll talk to you later."

TY WAS THRILLED that Rocco had come early. He'd meant it when he said the man was a perfect mix of tactical genius and suave diplomat. The combination was unusual, but it had served Rocco well.

The Blackout gang here might be able to use a little of his diplomacy now.

Ty quietly slipped from the apartment. He knew Cassidy had been sincere when she'd said she was okay with him leaving. In fact, having some time alone might do a world of wonders for her right now.

He slipped downstairs to where the Blackout offices were located. Colton and Rocco chatted in the lobby area. Rocco had a cup of coffee in hand.

The man had always been able to drink coffee, no matter what time of day it was, and still been able to sleep at night. Like a bear, if Ty remembered correctly.

Ty paused for a moment, wondering exactly how much he should tell the man about the current situation. The rest of the Blackout guys knew the truth about Cassidy. Did Rocco need to know also?

Ty knew he could trust him. He and Colton wouldn't have hired the man if they couldn't.

He sat down in a chair across from his friend, grabbing a water bottle from the hospitality table.

"I hear you guys have had quite the eventful day here." Rocco leaned back and took a sip of his drink.

Colton must have updated him. However, Ty knew that Colton wouldn't have shared Cassidy's secret.

"Yes, we have." Ty's jaw hardened as the turn of events replayed in his mind. "I'm afraid the FBI is targeting my wife for a crime she didn't commit."

Rocco frowned. "You know I'm here for you if you need anything."

"I appreciate that, man."

Ty wished this was a casual meeting. That they could simply catch up on old times. But Ty had too much on his mind to do that.

Ty glanced over as Griff stepped into the lobby.

Based on the man's stormy expression, this wasn't a social visit.

Griff paused in front of them. "I just found Kujo at the door."

Ty's dog, a golden retriever, bound into the room. If an animal could look proud of himself, that's exactly how Kujo could be described now.

"He seemed agitated when I found him, and I think he has something in his mouth," Griff continued. "I couldn't convince him to give it up."

"What?" Ty leaned down to get a better look.

Sure enough, the dog *did* have something in his mouth.

A piece of fabric.

Ty pulled on some gloves before taking the cloth from between the dog's teeth.

He held the swath up into the light for a better look. The dark blue, thin-weight material looked like it had been ripped from someone's pants or shirt.

Unease churned in Ty's gut.

"Did you know Kujo was outside?" Colton asked.

"I've been letting him wander the grounds for some extra security. Until now, it hasn't been a big deal."

"So if he ripped this from someone's clothes, then he pulled it from someone who's on these grounds . . ." Colton said.

Ty's jaw hardened. "We need to get our guys out there and see if we have an intruder."

"We do," Colton said. "And we don't have any time to waste."

CHAPTER SEVENTEEN

THE NEXT MORNING, Cassidy paused as she stared at Ty in the bathroom mirror. He told her what happened with Kujo last night.

"I can't believe you didn't wake me up to tell me that." She frowned before continuing to pull her hair back into a bun.

Ty shrugged and leaned against the bathroom counter. Annabeth was still sleeping and probably wouldn't wake up for another hour or so.

"You were sleeping, and I figured you needed your rest. Besides, we didn't find anything."

After she finished securing her hair, she crossed her arms, mimicking Ty's body language as she turned to face him. "How did someone get on campus? There are security cameras and fences. This place is secure.”

“That’s what we’re trying to figure out. There are a few dead zones, and we think that maybe someone got in either that way or through the water.”

Cassidy shook her head, not liking how this sounded. “That means we’re not even safe here.”

“If you’re here, you have a lot of people watching over you. Nobody can get inside the building without an ID. We just have to keep our eyes open.”

He had a point. But Cassidy still felt a headache coming on despite that. “Maybe we can analyze that swatch of fabric Kujo brought back. It could tell us something.”

“I thought you might say that.” Ty reached into his pocket and pulled out a bag with the fabric inside.

She took it from him. “Great minds think alike.”

“Yes, they do. There’s something else I want you to have.” He stepped out of the room before returning a moment later and placing an object in her hand.

Cassidy glanced at the item and squinted. “A burner phone?”

“I wouldn’t put it past the FBI to monitor your calls. If you need to get in touch with me, I want you to be able to do it. I have a burner phone also, and I programmed that number into your phone."

She slipped the phone into her back pocket. "Smart thinking. Thank you."

Ty shifted to lean in the doorway, already done with his five-minute morning routine. She still marveled that the man could shower, brush his teeth, and get dressed in that amount of time.

"What are you going to do today?" Ty asked.

"I need to go into the station. I want to confirm Governor Hollick's alibi and do a little more research on DH-7. Given all the restrictions the FBI has given me, there's not much else I can do. Anything with Samuel appears to be off-limits."

"Looking into Hollick and DH-7 sounds like a good idea," Ty said. "I'll be doing some work here and see if I can figure out if anyone unusual has been in town. Bethany already said Annabeth could stay with her today. She has a doctor's appointment, but CJ offered to fill in so she could go."

Cassidy frowned when she heard Annabeth's name. "I hate that we're not able to spend more time with her right now."

"I know, but she's safe and she's happy. Besides, if we're going to find out what's going on, we have no choice. Until we know all the details, we need to make sure that she's protected."

Cassidy nodded. Ty's words were true. But that didn't stop guilt from filling her.

The best thing Cassidy could do right now was to find the person responsible for these crimes.

Because no one would be safe until she did.

THE TENSION inside the police station couldn't be ignored. Tautness snapped through the air with every movement and every spoken word.

On one side of the strain was the FBI, who'd commandeered the conference room. On the other side was Cassidy and her officers. Even though her people knew not to speak of what was going on, she still felt the questions in the air.

Whatever she did, Cassidy couldn't let on to the FBI that they were disobeying direct orders from them.

After nodding to a couple of people, Cassidy slipped into her office. She had several calls she needed to make. Had the FBI bugged her office phone also? She didn't know. It was a possibility, she supposed.

When her door was locked, she picked up her desk phone and examined it. Best she could tell, there were no bugs on it.

Besides, even if someone was listening to everything she had to say, she didn't plan on sharing anything incriminating.

The first order on her agenda was to look up any information she could on Governor Hollick. Cassidy knew better than to call his office and ask for confirmation. But usually with the governor, his schedule was fairly public.

After a few minutes of research, she confirmed that Hollick had been on the western side of North Carolina on the day Samuel had died. He'd been meeting with some legislators there as well as campaigning for a man running for state attorney general. The evidence was irrefutable.

Next, Cassidy tried to track down Alexandria Manchester again.

She still had no luck. That fact left her feeling the most unsettled. Why didn't anyone know where the woman was? *Someone* knew *something*. Cassidy just had to find that person.

Had Alexandria gone into witness protection for some reason? But what sense would that make? Alexandria wouldn't go into a program like that without her daughter. At least, that was the sense that Cassidy got from the woman.

With a sigh, Cassidy stared at her phone. There was one more phone call she needed to make. Perhaps this one was the most critical.

After another moment of hesitation, she picked up the phone and dialed a man named Nicolas Thompson. Cassidy had worked with him back in Seattle, where he was the head of the gang unit.

The man, along with all her former colleagues, thought she was dead.

She was going to have to be very careful how to approach the conversation. But Nicolas, if anyone, would have the answers she needed.

The only catch was, Cassidy couldn't reveal who she really was.

The man was sharp. Would she be able to fool him?

She was about to find out.

CHAPTER EIGHTEEN

"CAPTAIN THOMPSON, my name is Cassidy Chambers, and I'm a police chief in North Carolina on an island called Lantern Beach."

"What can I do for you, Chief?"

Hearing his voice swept Cassidy back in time. He had that slight Seattle accent that reminded her so much of home. When she'd been assigned to the task force to bring down DH-7, it had felt like such an honor.

She forced her thoughts back to the present.

"We're investigating a crime here, and I understand that you're one of the leading experts on DH-7."

"That's right," Thompson said. "I have a lot of experience with them. What do you need to know?"

"Fortunately for us, we don't have many members of the gang living in this area."

"They're mostly based out of the West Coast, though, for a time, they'd started to spread toward the Midwest. I haven't heard much of them being out in North Carolina. Not since . . ."

Cassidy's lungs froze. She thought she knew what he was about to say, but she didn't want to jump to any conclusions. "Since?"

"Since they killed one of the finest detectives that I've ever met. She was in North Carolina when there was a hit on her. Several key gang leaders were arrested for it."

She forced her mouth to move, despite the shock sweeping through her. She hadn't been forgotten.

Hearing that brought her a surprising comfort.

"I'm sorry to hear that," Cassidy finally said. "I know that must be hard."

"We all felt it here at the department. Detective Matthews gave up a lot in order to protect us and to make our streets safer. She didn't deserve to die that way."

"No, I'm sure she didn't. Perhaps that's what makes it even more important that we make sure these guys aren't here. What can you tell me about the progression of DH-7 through the years? Are they still growing?"

"It's funny that you ask that," Thompson said. "The group has actually splintered. That information hasn't been made public."

"I hadn't heard that." Cassidy's pulse pounded. Could it be true?

"That's right. Members had a big disagreement after the death of their leader, Raul Sanders. Eventually, that led to a split."

Her pulse continued to race with subdued excitement. "I see. Would you say the split has weakened them as a whole?"

"I'd say they've weakened significantly. I'm sure you've heard the saying 'united we stand, and divided we fall'? Well, divided these guys are definitely coming apart at the seams."

That was the best news Cassidy had heard in a long time. "Do you have reason to think that any members may have traveled to this area?"

"I don't see why they would have. Most of the people who were loyal to Sanders have been arrested. He had a few core members, but the rest just kind of went underground and looked for someone to give them orders. It's been a few years now, and people have moved on."

"That's good, right?"

"I'd definitely say that's good news. Does this help you at all?"

"As a matter of fact, it does. It's been very helpful. Thank you so much for your assistance."

"It's no problem. I hope whatever problem you're dealing with out there can be resolved."

"Me too. Me too." Maybe—just maybe—Cassidy had one less problem to deal with right now.

CASSIDY NEEDED to talk to Ty and give him the update. Plus, she wanted to ask if he'd learned anything.

But she didn't want to make that phone call from her office. Instead, she stepped outside and paced toward her SUV where she might have some privacy.

But before she could even dial anything on her phone, the same reporter from yesterday appeared —Tina Andrews. Just as before, she wore a business suit and heels. Her dark hair was pulled into a neat ponytail.

But it was her eyes that caught Cassidy's attention. Her gaze was determined and stubborn without an ounce of warmth mixed with the ambition.

Was the woman stalking Cassidy?

Either way, Cassidy's irritation turned into annoyance.

"Are you ready to give me a comment yet?" Tina shoved a recorder toward her.

Cassidy glanced at the woman and narrowed her eyes. "No, I'm not."

"The public deserves to know what's going on here on this island. Why two FBI agents have been killed here over the past eight days."

"I'm afraid I can't answer that question." Cassidy reached for the door to her SUV.

Tina pushed herself in front of it before Cassidy could open it, surprisingly strong considering her thin build. "I'm not going to take no for an answer."

Cassidy bristled. "Are you going to make me arrest you?"

"I haven't done anything. I'm just having a conversation. Besides, this parking lot is public property. I'm not even trespassing."

Cassidy turned toward her, tired of this woman's pushy attitude. "I don't know who you think you are. But you need to get out of my way."

The woman stared at her a moment as if contemplating her next move. Finally, she pushed herself away from Cassidy's vehicle and nodded. "I hear you. But I'm not done."

Cassidy didn't say anything. She simply opened the door to her SUV and slammed it shut.

On second thought, she would go talk to Ty in person.

CHAPTER NINETEEN

TY HAD SPENT the morning combing the streets and looking for evidence, but he hadn't been successful at finding any.

Instead, he'd come back to the headquarters to talk to his guys and brainstorm.

He'd checked on Annabeth. Bethany had gone to see Doc Clemson for a pregnancy checkup. Another agent here, a woman named CJ Compton, was watching Annabeth and Ada.

His guys had been questioning all their new hires and trying to figure out who Kujo might have gone after last night. So far, they'd had no luck.

Ty ran his hand over his face. More than anything in this world, he wanted to protect his wife.

But the task seemed like it was getting harder all the time.

Ty looked up as someone charged into his office.

CJ.

Her eyes were wide and her motions jerky as she stopped in front of him. That said a lot considering the fact that CJ was never frazzled.

"It's Annabeth . . . she's gone." Her voice trailed with apprehension.

Ty jumped to his feet, unsure if he'd heard correctly. "What do you mean?"

"I mean, one minute we were playing in the lobby." CJ's voice climbed in pitch—something very unlike the normally even-keeled agent. "I went to the bathroom just for a minute. But when I got back, the window was open, and Annabeth was gone."

Ty rushed toward the door. "Did you look outside for her?"

CJ nodded, following beside him. "I ran out there, hoping I'd see her. But it was like she was never here. I promise, I was only in the bathroom for probably two minutes. I'm not sure how she got away that quickly."

Ty had a feeling he knew the answer to that question.

It was because someone on these grounds wasn't on the up and up.

"Where's Ada?" he asked. "Did she see anything?"

"Bethany just got back and took the girl upstairs. I thought that was the safest place she could be. And, no, she didn't see anything."

Ty hurried toward the lobby. "We need to get the guys to help us search. We don't have any time to waste."

"I'll let everyone know." CJ jogged toward the offices where the Blackout agents were.

Ty's heart raced as he paused in the lobby and glanced around.

What if someone had gotten Annabeth? Would they harm the girl?

He prayed that wasn't the case.

In fact, he prayed that this was all a misunder-standing.

But deep inside, he knew that it wasn't.

***

CASSIDY FROZE when she saw Ty dart into the lobby. Urgency captured his movements.

Something was wrong, she realized.

She dashed toward him. "What's going on?"

He took her arm and kept moving toward the door. "Annabeth is missing."

"What?" The word came out as a gasp.

He filled her in on what had happened as they rushed outside.

"Do you think she just ran away?" Cassidy tried to put together a picture of what had happened.

Ty stormed across the grass, scanning everything as he went. "I'm guessing that maybe someone lured her outside."

A sick feeling pooled in Cassidy's gut. She didn't like the sound of that.

Ty stopped and scooped up something from the ground.

A teddy bear. Just like the one Annabeth had in her room, only newer.

Someone must have known that.

Had this person stood outside the window and held up the bear?

Some of Cassidy's nausea turned into anger.

They had to find Annabeth.

Now.

"Annabeth!" she yelled, hoping the girl might hear her.

There was no response.

She knelt on the ground where the teddy bear had been found. Indentions were pressed into the grass. Two sets of them.

"Come on!" She motioned for Ty to follow.

The two of them tracked the steps toward the water.

It was the only area on this campus that wasn't secure. The rest of the facility had a fence around it.

That was why they had a security guard monitoring this area twenty-four/seven.

Had someone slipped past?

Ty and Cassidy took off into a run.

Just as they reached the sandy edge of the Pamlico Sound, they spotted a boat in the distance.

The vessel charged away from the shore, the figures aboard too far away to make out any details.

"Annabeth . . ." Cassidy muttered.

She grabbed her phone.

She had to call in backup and let people know what happened.

But before she could, a text message appeared on her screen.

Tell any other officers or the FBI and the little girl will die. More instructions are coming.

CHAPTER TWENTY

THE TEAM from Blackout put two boats in the water to begin a coastal search.

All Cassidy wanted was to call backup. But she felt certain the threat was real, and she couldn't risk telling anyone what was going on. She wouldn't do anything to put Annabeth in any more danger.

But the decision clawed at any sense of peace.

Griff, Dez, and Benjamin were in one boat headed north. Ty, Cassidy, and Colton were in the other heading south.

Cassidy would like to think the boat with Annabeth on it couldn't have gotten very far. But the truth was, it could have.

That boat could have gone out in the ocean. It could have gone up north to Ocracoke. It could have gone south to Emerald Isle. It could have even circled back around to the other side of the island. The possibilities seemed endless.

The thought wasn't comforting.

Cassidy stood near the cockpit, her gaze searching the horizon.

The wind blew against them, surprisingly chilly for the spring day. Cassidy let it sweep over her. Moisture misted from her eyes. She wasn't sure if the dampness was tears or something caused by the elements. Either way, she wiped the mist away with the back of her hand.

Ty's hand went to her waist as they stood together, searching the horizon. "We're going to find her."

Cassidy wished she felt so certain.

Two hours later, the boat was nowhere to be located.

The team met back near the dock at the Blackout headquarters where the other boat shared the same report.

The people who'd taken Annabeth had disappeared.

The thought echoed in Cassidy's head until she felt everything around her beginning to spin. She closed her eyes and righted herself. She couldn't let herself get emotional. It would only hurt her right now.

Ty paced the shore as he addressed the team. "We need to figure out who on campus could have either done this or helped with it. This was an inside job."

"We hired more people to work maintenance, in the kitchen, and with housecleaning," Colton said. "We've been questioning but have come up with nothing."

"We need to question them again." Ty's jaw flexed as he stared at each person in the circle, his gaze leaving no room for argument. "The sooner we know who might be behind this, the sooner we can make progress. Annabeth's life may depend on it."

"Should we call the FBI?" Griff asked.

"Normally, in situations like this, the answer would be yes," Cassidy said. "But we can't risk it. These people have already proven they're deadly. It's a chance we can't take."

"We have friends with helicopters," Dez said. "I'm sure they would help."

Ty and Cassidy glanced at each other before Ty finally spoke. "If we can keep this in-house, I think it will be better. For Annabeth's sake. You know I want to do everything I can to find her. But . . ."

Cassidy squeezed his hand.

He couldn't finish the statement.

Cassidy knew why. He couldn't stand the thought of anything happening to Annabeth. Neither could Cassidy.

The team split up and left Ty and Cassidy alone. When everyone else was gone, Ty pulled Cassidy into his arms and held her. Cassidy felt herself melting in his embrace.

"I can't believe we let this happen," Cassidy murmured, her mind still reeling. "I should have stayed here. I shouldn't have gone into work. Especially after Kujo brought back that piece of fabric—"

"It's not your fault. We were doing everything we can to help Annabeth."

"But I should have seen this—"

"No one can see into the future," Ty said. "I would have never thought someone might come to the window to try to lure her away."

Cassidy buried herself in Ty's arms. "I feel like everything is falling apart."

"The good news is that even when things fall apart, they eventually can be put back together. Don't ever forget that. Okay?"

She nodded in his arms, even though she wasn't sure if she truly believed the words.

But right now, they had to keep looking for Annabeth.

She would have time to wallow in her guilt later.

AN HOUR LATER, each of Blackout's new employees had been questioned again. No one was missing. Each of their uniforms had been checked.

No one seemed to know anything about what had happened.

But Ty knew that was impossible. He felt certain somebody working for Blackout had assisted in the abduction. It was the only scenario that made sense.

Even though he'd told Cassidy she had no reason to feel guilty, guilt tried to consume him also. He should have stayed with Annabeth. He should have anticipated something like this might happen.

But beating himself up would only serve to slow him down right now.

Everyone at Blackout had been confined in the main lodge until Ty figured out what was happening. No one was leaving until they had some answers.

Cassidy had been on her burner phone, calling various boaters she knew and asking them to be on the lookout. Boaters weren't the police, but she was still taking a gamble. Despite that, no one knew anything.

Ty stood to walk toward her. But before he reached her, her phone rang. She put it on speaker so he could hear.

"Hey, Paige," Cassidy started. "What's going on?"

"I thought you'd want to know that someone reported a dead body floating in one of the salt ponds not far from here."

"What?" Cassidy gasped as she glanced up at Ty and shook her head.

"I figured you'd want to get to the scene ASAP. I don't know if this is connected to the other recent crimes on the island but . . ."

"Thanks, Paige."

As Cassidy ended the call, she turned to Ty.

No words were needed.

He knew exactly what she was thinking.

When would the hits stop coming?

CHAPTER TWENTY-ONE

CASSIDY STEPPED TOWARD THE DOOR. "I have to go."

She didn't want to leave. She wanted to stay here. To strategize on how to find Annabeth. To await those instructions that were supposed to be coming.

But she was at the abductor's mercy.

She hated it. Waiting was the last thing she wanted. In other circumstances, she'd call the Coast Guard, the marine police, the state police—anyone she could.

But doing so now would put Annabeth's life in danger.

Plus, if she stayed away from this crime scene, people would start asking questions.

Her head throbbed at the thought.

Ty kept in stride with her as she stepped outside, headed toward her SUV. "Let me go with you."

"You should stay and take care of matters here. I have to handle this. If I bring anyone with me, it's only going to make things more suspicious."

He stared at her another moment as if uncertain about her words. Then he finally nodded. "I'll deal with things here. Be careful, and call me if you need me."

"I will." She quickly kissed his cheek before climbing into her SUV and pulling away.

Bradshaw was already at the scene securing the area when she arrived.

Two people stood in the background.

Cassidy squinted. Was that Serena Lavinia and Webster Newsome?

Serena had bought the ice cream truck from Cassidy when she'd become police chief. Webster was Serena's boyfriend and the local newspaper editor.

She waved to them before approaching Bradshaw at the edge of the murky water.

The scent of the salt pond rose around her—briny and slightly putrid. The wind blew, and the reeds surrounding the water brushed together as if warning them to stay away.

Cassidy glanced out over the dark water—water filled with lily pads and logs lined with turtles and a gaggle of geese.

Several feet away, she spotted something floating. Bradshaw had used a fishing pole to hold the body near the shore and prevent it from floating out farther.

"What happened?" she asked Bradshaw.

"Those two were out trying to find a good spot to take pictures for Instagram. Serena thought she saw something unusual floating in the pond, so she went to investigate. Lo and behold, it was a body. Based on what I could tell from a distance, he's been shot."

Cassidy's stomach clenched. "We're going to need to pull the body in."

"That's what I assumed. I hope you don't mind, but I took the liberty of calling Dillinger and Banks already."

"Smart move. I've been a little distracted." As the words left her lips, Annabeth's image filled her mind.

Where was the girl now? Was she okay? Was she scared?

If anyone hurt her . . . Cassidy fisted her hands at the mere thought of it. She wanted to be out there searching. Someone had known that and had wanted to stop her. That's why they'd sent that threat.

"As anyone would be in your shoes," Bradshaw said quietly.

Bradshaw thought her biggest worry was Samuel's death, she realized. He had no idea that Annabeth was missing. That seemed a tragedy in itself.

A few minutes later, Dillinger and Banks arrived. Doc Clemson also showed up. Cassidy halfway expected the FBI to ride onto the scene also, but they didn't.

Shortly after, the victim had been pulled out and laid on shore. Doc Clemson began his examination.

Their John Doe was probably in his forties. He appeared tall, and he'd probably been thin. Currently, water bloated his body and wrinkled his skin, making it nearly unrecognizable.

After photographing him, Cassidy slipped on some gloves and reached into his pocket.

He had a wallet on him.

She opened it, looking for a way to ID the man.

But when she saw the name on the driver's license, she sucked in a breath.

Ronnie Baskins.

That was the name of the new maintenance worker at Blackout.

But if this man was the real Ronnie Baskins . . . then someone may have killed him in order to take his position on the campus.

Cassidy grabbed her phone. She had to call Ty and warn him.

"RONNIE BASKINS IS DEAD."

Everything went still around Ty as Cassidy's words echoed in his mind. Even though the lobby was full of the Blackout support staff, he hardly heard any of their chatter. Instead, his gaze searched the crowd for their newest maintenance worker.

Everybody who'd been hired to work at Blackout was vetted. They'd had background checks. Character witnesses. Flawless résumés.

Considering the work done here, Ty and Colton had no choice but to go through those measures, including for groundskeepers and housekeeping staff.

Yet someone had managed to bypass their system by killing a new employee and acting as an imposter. Why had it been so important to plant someone inside the Blackout campus?

He didn't know, but fury churned inside him at the thought.

As Ty pulled the phone away from his ear, he heard Cassidy saying something about being on the way and not doing anything rash.

He knew what she was getting at.

Cassidy feared Ty might do something he'd regret.

And he just might.

His gaze zeroed in on the man who went by the name Ronnie. How had the man passed himself off as the real Ronnie? The two looked remarkably similar. Ty had been there when Colton had interviewed him.

Whoever this man really was, he was good. He'd even adopted the real Ronnie's mannerisms and speech patterns.

Ty stormed across the lobby, ready to get some answers.

"Ty?" Colton muttered as he walked past.

Ty hardly heard him.

The fake Ronnie glanced up from where he talked to a housekeeper in the corner. When he spotted Ty, he froze.

He knew he'd been made.

The next instant, the man reached behind him and drew a gun. "Stay back!"

Everyone froze where they were.

Ty didn't have to turn around to know that Colton and Griff had already pulled their own guns.

Imposter Ronnie was outnumbered.

Ty stepped closer, all too aware of the gun in the man's hands. But he couldn't let that stop him. "Where's Annabeth? What did you do with her?"

"I don't know what you're talking about."

"Don't play games," Ty continued. "Where is she?"

The man said nothing.

Ty let out a breath, trying to keep a grip on his emotions. "You don't remember that information? Fine. Tell us who you really are."

"My name is Ronnie." The gun trembled in the man's hand.

"You're not Ronnie. You killed Ronnie, and you abducted Annabeth. Let's stop playing games."

Defiance flashed in the man's eyes. "I don't have to talk to you."

Ty curled his hand into a fist. His fighting instincts tried to claw their way to the surface. He wanted more than anything to lunge forward. To grasp this man by his neck. To demand answers.

But there were too many other people around. Innocent people. He couldn't risk anybody getting hurt.

Still, Ty knew that time was of the essence.

"You're not going to walk away from here, *Ronnie*." Ty made it clear he knew that wasn't his real name. "Why don't you just put the gun down, and we can have a conversation?"

"That's not going to happen." The man's voice cracked with anger—and fear.

Ty needed to somehow get this man talking, but he was quickly losing his patience. "What's your real name?"

"There's no need to keep questioning me. You won't get anything out of me." Satisfaction replaced his anger and fear.

"I beg to differ. You need to put the gun down. You know if you pull the trigger that you're not going to walk away from this alive."

"Is that right?"

The next instant, gunfire exploded in the room.

Ty braced himself as he tried to figure out who had pulled the trigger . . . and who might have been hurt.

CHAPTER TWENTY-TWO

CASSIDY RUSHED into the Blackout building just as she heard gunfire.

She dashed toward the lobby. But she stopped in her tracks when she saw the scene there.

Colton and Griff both had their guns drawn. Ty knelt on the floor beside someone.

Support staff scrambled behind furniture and stared with fear at the scene.

Cassidy's gaze stopped at a man sprawled on the floor.

Ty shook his shoulders. "What did you do with Annabeth? Tell us."

Cassidy rushed toward them, trying to figure out exactly what had happened here.

The man's eyes were still open.

He was barely hanging on.

But he was alive.

The man opened his mouth as if he were going to say something.

Ty leaned closer.

Cassidy knelt on the other side. This man had something to do with Annabeth's abduction. He had answers, answers they desperately needed.

The man's lips moved, but no words emerged.

What was he trying to say?

"Where is she?" Ty demanded again.

The man's lips moved again. But his eyes were becoming more glazed with each second.

He tried to whisper something.

Ty leaned closer. "What? Where is she?"

Cassidy held her breath, waiting for him to respond.

Praying for answers.

The man gasped as if trying to speak.

Then a laugh sounded.

The man thought this was funny. Thought their hope was amusing.

This guy was taunting them.

Ty's eyes narrowed as he stared down at the man. Through clenched teeth, he muttered, "I don't know what kind of game you're playing—"

But before Ty could finish that statement, the man's eyes went blank.

He was dead.

And they still didn't have any answers.

"I NEED EVERYONE TO REMAIN CALM," Cassidy said. "Griff, help me get everyone out of here and into the conference room. I'll need to question them. But first, I need to document this scene and call the paramedics."

The man was clearly dead but protocol was protocol.

She stared at the man sprawled on the floor and frowned. He'd enjoyed dying without giving them any answers. The thought disgusted her.

Cassidy had two dead bodies on her hands now.

She and her crew hadn't even finished investigating the other scene, and now this.

She walked toward Ty, grateful he was okay. But now she needed to get to the bottom of what had transpired here. "What happened?"

Ty glared at the man, his upper lip twitching with disgust. "I started to confront him when he pulled out a gun. Colton and Griff were both with me. The man seemed to realize he wasn't going to get out of the situation, and he turned the gun on himself."

Cassidy shook her head, the sickly feeling in her stomach coupled with an oncoming headache. This wasn't the way she wanted things to go—on so many levels.

"He could have given us answers." Ty rubbed his jaw, obviously frustrated. "He could have told us where Annabeth was. Who was that guy anyway? Who is he really?"

"That's what we need to figure out."

Ty let out a sigh before his gaze fell on Cassidy. Some of his focus seemed to return. "How can we help?"

"We need to search the room where this man was staying and see if there's anything that will tell us who he really is," Cassidy said.

"I can do that."

"I'll search his phone and computer if he has one. Maybe something there will tell us his real name. But in the meantime, I need to secure the scene. I'm going to have to take statements as well. Even though the man shot himself, I still need to handle this as an official police investigation."

"Of course." His voice dropped. "I'm . . . sorry. I didn't think this would happen."

Cassidy nodded, even though part of her felt numb. "I know. I know."

The thought of that little girl being out there alone and without her caused unseen burdens to crush Cassidy's heart. If she let herself, she might totally lose it. She hadn't realized just how close she'd become to Annabeth since the two had met. But Cassidy had felt like it was her personal responsibility to look out for the girl.

And she'd failed.

Just like she seemed to be failing this town right now.

But she was going to turn things around—if it was the last thing she did.

CHAPTER TWENTY-THREE

CASSIDY HAD no choice but to call Watkins.

She'd hoped this wouldn't be the case. But with two dead bodies on the island just today and Samuel's earlier death, she knew it would only make things worse if she kept this from him.

As she waited for him to arrive, she gathered evidence, photographed the scene, and took statements. Banks came to the Blackout complex to help her in that process while Bradshaw and Dillinger continued at the scene near the marsh.

Mac had also shown up to offer his assistance.

Despite that, all Cassidy really wanted to do was to find Annabeth. She couldn't stop thinking about the little girl.

She wanted to use all her time and resources to

get out there and find her. But she had no doubt that the person who'd left that threatening message was telling the truth. If Cassidy told law enforcement about what happened, they would hurt the girl.

Cassidy couldn't risk that.

Her phone rang. She saw Gail Kline's number. What did the social worker in charge of Annabeth's case want?

More dread filled her stomach as she put the phone to her ear, but she tried to force herself to sound cheerful. "Hey, Gail. How are you?"

"Cassidy!" Gail started. "I know this is last minute, but I wanted to let you know that I'm headed your way."

Cassidy's lungs froze. "Come again?"

"That's right. I had to come over to Lantern Beach to do something else, so I'm just going to stop in to do a home check on Annabeth."

Cassidy tried to keep her voice neutral. "This isn't a great time. We actually just had an incident here at the Blackout complex that we're dealing with and—"

"Is Annabeth okay?" Gail rushed.

Again, Cassidy's chest squeezed. "Annabeth wasn't involved in this incident."

It was the truth. But Cassidy still felt rotten as she skirted around the woman's question.

Telling her would get Annabeth taken away. And having her taken away could put her in even more danger.

Still, Cassidy always preferred the truth.

"Well, that's a relief." Gail let out a chuckle. "But I'd really like to come check on her myself. I gotta keep things official, you know."

Cassidy knew she couldn't put Gail off for too much longer. It would only make the woman more suspicious. But what did she say?

She was a police chief. She should have the answers to things like this. But she didn't. This wasn't something she'd trained for.

"I'll see you in about ten minutes," Gail announced.

The call ended before Cassidy could argue.

Cassidy had to figure out a way to handle this situation—a way to handle it without Annabeth getting hurt.

Her mind raced.

"Speaking of Annabeth . . . where *is* the girl?" someone said behind her.

Cassidy turned and saw Watkins standing there, eyeing her suspiciously.

He'd heard part of that conversation, hadn't he?

As she stared at the man, she realized she needed to make a split-second decision. A split-second decision that could change the outcome of this whole case—for better or worse.

***

CASSIDY LICKED HER LIPS. *Dear Lord, I don't know what to do right now. I could really use some wisdom.*

She wished she could quickly consult with Ty or Mac and get their feedback. But there was no time for that. Watkins waited for her answer, an impatient —and possibly a gotcha!—look in his gaze.

She sucked in a deep breath.

Tell Watkins and risk Annabeth possibly being in greater danger?

Or stay quiet and make up an excuse?

Sweat covered her palms.

She glanced behind Watkins and saw his rookie agent, Rohl, lingered there. Listening. Watching. Observing.

Cassidy turned her gaze back to Watkins. "Annabeth's taking a nap. I don't want to wake her."

Watkins' eyes remained narrow. "Why do I feel like you're hiding something from us?"

"Why don't we just concentrate on what's going on here right now?"

"I would *love* to concentrate on what's going on right now. But what I want to know is why someone who was supposed to be working at the Blackout facility was killed and somebody else took his place. What aren't you telling me, Cassidy Chambers?"

At just that moment, Ty appeared beside her. He bristled near Watkins, stepping just barely in front of Cassidy. "Are we under investigation?"

Watkins took a slight step back. "No. Should you be?"

"We're a company made up of former Navy SEALs. We have a long list of people we've made angry, so there are endless reasons why somebody may have wanted to sneak onto this campus."

Watkins looked unimpressed as he continued to scowl. "Do you have any idea who this man was?"

"No, we don't," Ty said. "But believe me, my guys and I will be looking into this just as fervently as anybody. Incidents like this aren't acceptable."

Watkins let out a skeptical grunt while taking notes.

In the middle of jotting down something, his cell phone beeped, and he looked at the screen for several moments. Uneasiness jostled inside Cassidy as she waited to see if Watkins had an update.

Was he taking so long in order to make them sweat? She wouldn't put it past him.

Finally, he looked up, a new calmness in his eyes.

"One of our tech guys just discovered something on Stephens' phone," he started.

"What's that?" Cassidy knew there was a good chance that Watkins wouldn't tell her, but she asked anyway.

"One of the apps was actually what's known as a hiding app. It looks like a calculator, but actually there are messages hidden there."

"Anything that will tell us who killed him?"

Watkins locked his gaze with Cassidy. "From what I just read, yes, that is the case."

"That's great news. Who do you think killed him?"

Watkins' eyes locked on hers. "You. Those messages were from you."

CHAPTER TWENTY-FOUR

CASSIDY FELT HERSELF REELING. That hadn't been what she'd expected to hear.

"You've got this wrong." She shook her head. "I told you the truth when I said I'd only spoken to him once recently."

"You never did tell me what you guys were working in conjunction with."

Cassidy shrugged. "Like I said, it was between Samuel and me. Apparently, he doesn't have a direct supervisor. I tried to contact someone, but I came up empty."

Watkins said nothing. Did that mean Cassidy was right?

Cassidy felt Ty bristling beside her as the two men stared off. She placed her hand on his arm, urging him to calm down. The way Watkins looked triggered right now, it wouldn't surprise her if the man was looking for an excuse to arrest any of them.

"What did these so-called messages say?" Cassidy asked.

"You asked him to come here. Asked him to meet you in those woods. Said you had matters to discuss."

Cassidy's jaw tightened. "I didn't send those messages."

"So how did they get on his phone?" Watkins asked.

"I'm being set up. Somebody wants to make me look guilty. That's why I was called out to the woods to look for somebody who wasn't there. Somebody knew that I was going to be out there at the same time as Samuel. They want you looking at me so you don't look at them. Why can't you see that?"

"Why is there no recording of the 911 call?"

Cassidy swallowed hard. He'd done his home-work. "Someone called my line directly. It's clear now why they did that, but, in a small town, it's not entirely that unusual."

Watkins clicked his tongue. "Very convincing. But quite elaborate, don't you think? The most obvious suspect is you. Once we comb through these texts, I think we're going to have an imminent arrest on our hands."

Cassidy's stomach dropped. He was talking about her.

Her head spun at the thought of it.

———

CASSIDY TOOK a moment to compose herself. But her mind continued to race as his words echoed again and again.

We're going to have an imminent arrest on our hands.

She didn't have much time, did she?

That meant she needed answers. And she needed them now. "I know I've already asked you this once, but where is Alexandria Manchester? Are you ready to admit the truth yet?"

Watkins flinched as if he hadn't been expecting that question. "She's in jail waiting for the legal process to play out. Why?"

"Like I said before, I called the jail. She's not there. I need to know where she is."

"I don't see what this has to do with anything." His expression remained stony.

"It has *everything* to do with this." Cassidy kept

her voice hard to let him know she meant business. "Alexandria is a hacker. If the wrong person uses Alexandria's skills again, they can force her to do things for them. Things like planting evidence on an FBI agent's cell phone."

He stared at her a moment before letting out a chuckle. "That seems a bit overblown, don't you think?"

"As a matter of fact, no. I don't think it's overblown at all. The fact you're not answering my question only confirms that. Where *is* Alexandria?"

His jaw shifted back and forth.

Cassidy figured he would avoid her question again. She waited for a smart—or sharp—comeback.

Instead, he said, "Last I heard, she was transferred to a CIA facility."

Concern ricocheted through Cassidy. "A CIA facility? You can't just do that."

His jaw flexed. "It wasn't my call. That's all I know. They didn't tell me anything else, and I'm afraid it's not a matter I have any say in."

"Who is 'they'?"

He shrugged—or was that a squirm? "I'm not at liberty to say. But people above me made the call."

Cassidy shook her head, unable to believe what

she was hearing. "Can't you see Alexandria might be being victimized here? Where are you now when an innocent woman needs help?"

Watkins glowered down at her. "You need to keep yourself in check, Chief."

Cassidy was about to retort when Colton approached them. "Chief, there's someone at the gate to see you."

She swallowed her harsh words and tried to pull herself together.

She knew who was here.

Gail.

The social worker couldn't see her like this. She was too wound up.

"Please, excuse us," Cassidy muttered.

"Don't wander too far." Watkins' voice suddenly sounded more cheerful.

The last person Cassidy wanted to listen to was that man. But she knew if she didn't comply that he could make her life miserable.

A headache pounded in her temples at the thought.

CHAPTER TWENTY-FIVE

"WHAT'S GOING ON, CASSIDY?" Ty felt the pressure continue to build around them. "Who's here?"

Pressure tugged at him with enough force that he felt a tightness in his chest he hadn't felt in a long time.

Maybe even since he was a SEAL.

"Gail wants to do a home visit for Annabeth," Cassidy told him as they walked toward the gate. "She just called right before Watkins confronted me."

He sucked in a breath at the news. "Talk about awful timing. What are we going to do?"

"Remember the first time she came?" Cassidy slowed her steps as they headed down the gravel lane. "Remember how she talked about really loving Navy SEALs, so you distracted her for a little while?"

"I remember."

She glanced up at him. "Can you do that again?"

Ty's eyebrows shot up. "She's already seen the Blackout facility. What else am I supposed to do? Besides, I might be able to distract her for an hour. I wish I could believe we're going to get Annabeth back in that time period, but that's hardly the case."

"I know. I just need to figure out what we're going to do. I need you to buy some time."

Ty glanced at Cassidy and saw the stress pulling at her features. He didn't remember ever really seeing Cassidy like this before.

She was always so calm and in control. But clearly everything was getting to her. How could it not? This was too much for anyone to handle right now.

"We've got to find Annabeth," Ty said.

"I know." Cassidy lowered her voice. "But our guys are stretched thin with these other two dead bodies. I almost told Watkins that she was missing, but I don't know that I can trust him."

"I don't know that you can trust him either. He seems to have a vendetta against you. That other agent—I think his name is Rohl—might be a better bet."

"Maybe. So what do we do in the meantime?" Cassidy looked up at him, questions in her gaze.

Ty stared off in the distance before shaking his head. "Whoever abducted Annabeth said that they would be sending more instructions, right?"

"That's right."

"Then I guess we don't have any choice but to wait."

Cassidy frowned. "I hate waiting. What if she's hurt?"

"I know." He squeezed Cassidy's hand. "Believe me, I know. But I don't think they'll hurt her. Annabeth's not really the person they're targeting. For some reason, they want the feds to be focused on you."

"But why? That's what doesn't make sense in all this. I have nothing to offer. If DH-7 is behind this, then they would just kill me. But whoever is responsible for these crimes wants to make me suffer."

"Or they want to teach you a lesson. In the Middle East, people—terrorists—would beat other people down. They wanted to break their spirits. Once that happened, they were able to control their targets."

"So you think someone took Annabeth in order to control me?" She glanced in the distance and spotted Gail's car at the gate. She frowned at the sight of it.

"I think it's a good possibility. Maybe if they control you, they can frame you for something else. Something bigger than what we've seen right here."

Cassidy shook her head. "I don't even want to think about that."

Neither did Ty. But avoiding the truth would do nothing to help them. So he needed to think of every possibility.

But right now, he needed to deal with Gail.

AS CASSIDY LEFT Ty to handle Gail, she knew what she needed to do.

Officers, FBI agents, and Blackout members lingered outside the building. Some were working the scene. Others were here as backup.

She searched the group for Mac and pulled him aside. They stood close enough to the crowd to keep an eye on them but far enough away for privacy. Pine trees swayed above them, offering a surprisingly chilly shade considering the otherwise warm day.

Mac squinted as he turned to her. "What's going on?"

Cassidy frowned—but only for a moment—before announcing, "I need you to take over as police chief."

"What?" Shock coursed through his voice and surprise filled his gaze.

"Mac, I'm not in a position to deal with all this right now. The stakes are too personal, and I'm not going to make unbiased decisions."

"Cassidy . . ." His voice sounded wistful and uncertain.

"This is what needs to be done right now." Cassidy leaned closer before saying, "They took Annabeth."

Mac's eyes widened. "What? We need to organize teams and—"

"Whoever took her said if I told anyone else in law enforcement Annabeth would die. I can't put her at risk like that. I know the statistics. I've been in these situations before—just not with a child under my care. But I just can't take any chances right now."

"So what are you going to do?"

"This person who took her said to wait for more instructions."

"What about that dead body in the salt pond?

Someone killed the real Blackout employee and came here as an imposter?"

"That's my guess," Cassidy said. "This guy either let somebody into the facility who was able to lure Annabeth out. Or that man snatched Annabeth himself and took her to the boat before coming back to work."

"So when did this guy start here at the facilities?"

"Only three days ago," Cassidy said. "Ty and Colton vetted him. Of course, they had no idea that the real Ronnie Baskins was dead, and this guy was put here in his place."

Mac rubbed his jaw and stared into the distance a moment as if collecting his thoughts. "Whoever's behind this has money and connections. He had to know this guy was coming to work here. Then he found someone who looked strangely similar to come in his place."

"And did they do all this because of Annabeth? Was she the end goal? Or has this guy been doing other things around here at the Blackout facility?" Cassidy shook her head, wishing she had some answers. "And why did he risk coming back after assisting in Annabeth's abduction?"

"Those are great questions."

"My guys are checking it out now, making sure

there are no more surprises," Cassidy said. "I've got to find Annabeth. I know it's my duty to look into these two deaths that occurred on the island today. But there's no way I can give them my concentration. Not with Annabeth out there. That's why I need you to temporarily take over."

"Cassidy . . ." Mac shook his head. After a moment of what seemed like contemplation he finally nodded. "I'll do it. I'll step in for you. For now."

She frowned, knowing she wasn't done with her bad news yet. "There's one other thing you should know. There's a good chance that Watkins will arrest me. Someone planted evidence on Samuel's cell phone, evidence that makes it look like I was texting him. That I was the one who asked him to come out to the woods to meet me."

"It's still circumstantial."

"But these guys are looking for someone to blame, and they've got me in their sights."

"Do you think they're trying to frame you because one of them is involved? You said Stephens warned you not to trust Watkins."

"But Samuel never had a chance to explain that statement to me, so I don't know exactly what he was getting at. There's so much I don't know right now. I've never felt so uncertain, and I don't like it."

Mac patted her arm, compassion warming his gaze. "We're going to figure this out. One way or another, we will. I know you're under a lot of pressure right now. But don't give up."

Cassidy nodded. "I won't."

Especially not while Annabeth was out there.

CHAPTER TWENTY-SIX

CASSIDY STOOD in front of the doors outside the Daniel Oliver Building and announced to everyone that Mac would be taking over as police chief for the time being. Then she stepped back and let Mac field any further questions on how things would run from here on out.

Besides, she could use a moment to breathe. A moment alone. A moment away from Watkins.

She slipped around the corner of the building, out of sight from everyone, and leaned against the cedar-planked wall. She drew in several deep breaths as she tried to compose herself.

She was going to get through this. But she'd never forgive herself if something happened to Annabeth.

That girl was all she needed to concentrate on for the moment.

After Cassidy had taken a few more deep breaths, her phone buzzed. Her heart lurched when she heard the sound. Lately, the news on the other end hadn't been good.

Quickly, she pulled it from her pocket and glanced at the screen.

It was the same number the earlier message about Annabeth had been sent from.

There was a new message now.

Meet me on SW quadrant of Blackout property, other side of fence. Come now. Tell no one. If you do, the girl's blood will be on your hands. You have 10 minutes.

More nausea gargled in Cassidy's stomach.

She glanced around.

Nobody could see her from here. She could slip away without anyone knowing.

Besides, she couldn't tell Ty. Ty was with Gail. And she couldn't tell Mac because Mac was addressing everybody on the scene.

For that matter, maybe this was the perfect time to slip away.

She didn't have much time to think. Instead, she hurried toward the area the sender had told her to go.

When she got closer to the water, she remained near the fence until she found the gate there. She typed in the code on the lock, and it opened.

She looked back once more, but she knew nobody could see her. The building blocked that possibility, along with some scattered trees in the area.

Quickly, she locked the gate again before stepping into the woods.

According to the text, she needed to go south.

She followed a trail through the woods, unsure what to expect.

But she remained on guard. Anything could happen right now. She needed to be prepared.

Just as the thought went through her head, a stick broke in the distance.

She paused and braced herself for a possible attack. She reached for her gun.

That's when she saw a man lingering behind a tree about eight feet in front of her. He wore a mask so she couldn't see his face.

"Don't come any closer," Cassidy warned, still gripping her gun.

"I won't."

That was easier than she'd expected. She stiffened, suspicious about this man's intentions.

"What do you want?" she finally asked. "Where is Annabeth?"

"Not so fast."

"Please." Cassidy tried to control the desperation in her voice before that man heard it and used it against her. "What do you want from me?"

Before the man answered, she sensed a movement behind her. The next instant, something covered her mouth.

A sweet, almost acetone smell filled her nostrils.

Chloroform, she realized.

She fought, struggling against the man. But it was too late. The drug had already taken effect.

Everything around Cassidy went black.

"I THINK what you're doing here is great." Gail practically glowed as she looked around the wind-hewn landscape and let out a sigh.

The woman was in her mid-thirties with a stout build and bobbed brown hair. She clearly loved her job—and she loved Navy SEALs.

Ty kept Gail on the other side of the property, far away from the main building where police and the FBI had gathered. If she saw everyone there, she was sure to get suspicious, and he didn't want that.

Ty and his team had just started plans to build a little airstrip on the far side of their campus. Really, nothing had been done yet. But this was one area Gail hadn't seen last time she was here.

Buy time, he reminded himself. That was the most important thing he could do right now.

As they walked, Gail went on and on about some recent Navy SEAL movies she'd seen.

Ty glanced around at the woods in the distance and the water beyond it.

Where was Cassidy right now? The Blackout facilities were on the other side of the property. But if Ty looked through the trees, he caught glimpses of the Pamlico Sound.

Was somebody over there right now?

Whoever it was, they were too far away for him to be able to tell anything about them.

But Ty thought for sure he saw some type of movement.

Was it an investigator looking into what happened? Maybe one of the feds?

Or was it an operative who'd snatched Annabeth coming back to do more damage?

It would take a lot of guts for someone to come back right now. Ty didn't think that was the case.

But he had a burning desire to check it out. His gut told him he needed to.

Quickly, he texted Rocco and asked him to meet him. He knew just what he needed to do right now.

A few minutes later, Ty's friend strode toward him, a warm smile on his face. The diplomatic one of the group. The man who could charm anyone with his accent.

That would come in handy right now.

Gail giggled as soon as she saw him. "Who is this?"

"I'd like for you to meet our newest team member. This is Rocco Foster. Rocco, this is Gail, one of the best social workers here on the East Coast."

Gail giggled again. "Oh, you stop."

"I thought you might like to meet Rocco because he's one of America's finest as all the guys like to say. He's going to show you the new training course we set up, including a twenty-foot wall that he can scale in thirty seconds flat."

Rocco's eyes widened as he looked at him. Ty

might have been exaggerating slightly. And Rocco wasn't exactly dressed to scale the wall.

But his friend would think of something.

"I can't wait," Rocco said.

"I'm going to leave you two together for a minute so I can follow up on something," Ty said. "Is that okay?"

Gail seemed to remember why she was here and shook her head as she came back to reality. "I really should check on Annabeth ..."

"She's still napping so maybe it's better this way. Do you have to go back today?" Ty kept his voice casual.

"I was hoping to catch the ferry at six." She glanced at her watch.

"You have two whole hours then. No worries." Ty flashed another grin.

She thought about it a moment before nodding. "Fine then. Why not?"

But Ty wished he believed that no worries were possible.

Because all he felt right now was concern about one too many situations.

CHAPTER TWENTY-SEVEN

CASSIDY'S EYES JERKED OPEN. Her head felt groggy and her body sore.

Suddenly, what had happened hit her.

Those men had found her.

Drugged her.

Abducted her.

Where was she now?

She blinked as she waited for her vision to come into focus.

Darkness surrounded her. Wherever she was, the space was confined. Her knees were bent and her back was against something.

She moved her legs. No, the area was larger than she thought. Not large enough for her to stretch out, but she could move a little.

Carpet scraped her cheek and hands.

Then she heard the hum.

She noticed movement.

She was in a trunk, Cassidy realized. A car trunk, most likely.

And the car was moving, taking her somewhere.

Otherwise, silence stretched. No one talked in the front seat. Music didn't blare from a radio.

She glanced around again, wishing it wasn't so dark so she might see something. But she couldn't. Only blackness stared back.

How long had she been in here? From what she remembered, chloroform only lasted ten minutes or so, depending on a person's size and the dosage.

She blinked several times, trying to pull herself out of her dazed state. She needed to think clearly right now. Her life depended on it. Most likely, Annabeth's life did also.

She moved her arms. They weren't bound. Nor was her mouth taped shut.

Whoever had thrown her back here seemed confident she would remain here and wouldn't be a threat.

The thought didn't comfort her.

She felt around the edges of the space, searching

for a release switch to pop the trunk open. Most new cars had those.

But as her hands explored the darkness, there was nothing but carpet and the metal underside of the trunk door.

Was she in an old car?

She couldn't know for sure.

What else could she do?

She could kick out the taillight. Or she could look for a latch that might allow her to climb into the backseat.

First, she would try the taillight. It was daylight outside and climbing into the backseat might not work if the driver could easily see her.

Using her heel, Cassidy began kicking at the back of the light.

It wasn't as easy as she'd assumed.

But she wasn't going to give up yet. She'd give this a few more minutes and then she would try the backseat.

Cassidy kicked the taillight again. It came loose, but just a little.

Still, hope grew inside her.

She started to kick again when she felt the car slow. Then slow some more. And then slow even more.

Her breath caught.

What were these people doing? Where was she? And what was going to happen next?

A door opened. Probably the driver's.

Footsteps paced outside.

Cassidy held her breath as she waited for the trunk to open.

TY FOUND Colton milling outside the Blackout building and pulled him aside. "Have you seen Cassidy?"

"Not since Mac announced he was taking over as police chief."

Ty frowned. What had his friend just said? "Come again?"

Mac strode up to them as if he'd sensed what they were talking about. "Cassidy asked me to do so on a temporary basis. She said she couldn't be unbiased in this situation. I hate to say it, but I think it was a good call considering everything that's going on right now."

Ty could see where he was coming from. Everything was happening fast.

A bad feeling brewed in his gut.

He glanced from Colton to Mac. "But neither of you have seen her recently?"

"She slipped around the building as Mac was talking," Colton said. "I had the sense she needed some time alone. But I haven't seen her since then. I'll check with everyone and see if anybody has seen her lately."

"Please do," Ty said. "It's not like her to disappear without telling anyone."

Mac squinted as he stared at Ty. "You think something happened to her?"

Ty's heart pounded more quickly in his chest when he heard the words out loud. "I don't know. But we need to be certain. I thought I saw somebody over there past the fence. You wouldn't be able to see anything from here, but from the angle where I was standing, I saw someone. We need to check it out."

"I can help," Mac said.

"You need to be here and distract the FBI until we know what's going on. There's too much riding on this whole situation. But I'll get one or two of my guys to come help."

"That sounds fine. But you let me know if there's anything I can do. You know I would go through fire and water to help that girl."

"I know. And we appreciate that. I'll let you know." Ty started toward the fence.

Colton joined him again, falling in step beside him. "I sent a text to everyone. No one has seen Cassidy."

Ty frowned. He'd hoped for good news, though he hadn't expected it.

They hurried toward the back of the property, keeping their eyes open for any signs of trouble.

Once Ty reached the gated area near the water, he spotted the footprints on the ground.

He punched in the code and opened the gate before they stepped into the woods surrounding the property.

Footprints continued there also. He followed them, hoping they might find Cassidy.

But what had she been doing out here?

Ty longed to find her and ask her.

But as they continued to follow the trail, he stopped.

Two other sets of footprints were also here.

His heart pounded harder.

Colton looked up at him, squinting against the sunlight. "Do you think Cassidy met somebody here?"

"That's what I'm afraid of." Ty nodded to the

other side of the woods. "Let's keep following the trail."

They rushed through the woods, following the tracks.

But they stopped when Ty saw two sets of tire treads appear on a narrow opening through the trees.

Someone had snatched Cassidy, Ty realized.

Most likely, they'd put her in a vehicle.

And Ty had no idea where she might be.

But he had to find her.

CHAPTER TWENTY-EIGHT

CASSIDY HEARD footsteps crunching outside the car as if someone were walking around it toward the back.

But the trunk never opened.

What was going on out there?

She pounded her fist on the metal above her. "Hey! What are you doing! Let me out!"

Silence answered her.

She paused and held her breath, trying to hear what was happening.

Her heart pounded into her ears as dread—and adrenaline—filled her.

The next instant, the car began moving again—but just slightly.

Someone had clearly cut the engine. So what sense did the movement make?

Unless . . .

No, Cassidy couldn't think like that. That couldn't be what was about to happen. Someone wasn't pushing the car somewhere, leaving the motor off so no one would hear.

But obviously, they were.

Where could they possibly be pushing the car, though?

She pounded on the trunk again and began yelling. "Let me out! You're not going to get away with this!"

But just as she'd thought, no one responded.

She could try to kick out the taillight again, but she didn't think that would do her any good.

Instead, she turned to the seat behind her. She needed to figure out if she could get that seat down.

She felt around her, looking again for some type of trigger mechanism.

There was nothing.

If this was an older car, as she suspected it might be, then there was a chance there wasn't any type of mechanism. Could she somehow force the seat down?

She had no idea.

The car suddenly slowed.

Why was that?

Moving at what felt like a snail's pace, the car continued forward. And forward. And forward.

Then Cassidy heard a new sound—almost like the atmosphere around her had changed.

What was that? Was someone dousing the car with something? Some type of liquid? Were they going to set it on fire?

Adrenaline charged through her. There was no way she could survive that. She'd be burned alive.

She pounded on the trunk again. "Let me out! You don't have to do this!"

But this time, the sound of her fist hitting the metal seemed more muted. Almost as if she had been placed inside another kind of box or something.

Panic started to clutch her, but she pushed it back.

Not now.

She needed to keep a cool head.

Silence stretched, almost as if Cassidy were now in a cocoon of some sort.

She glanced at the taillight that she'd kicked out just an inch or so.

That's when she saw the water flooding into the space.

Someone had pushed the car into the water, she realized.

And if she didn't get out soon, this car would be her watery grave.

TY PULLED out his phone and called Bradshaw. "Are you busy?"

"You could say that," Bradshaw said. "We're still dealing with the dead body we found in the salt pond. What's going on?"

"We think somebody may have abducted Cassidy."

Bradshaw didn't say anything for a minute before muttering a shocked, "What?"

"We followed the tracks as far as we could," Ty said. "But a dog like Ranger could be really useful right now. Cassidy said he's able to even track a scent from a car."

Ranger was the first K9 officer Lantern Beach had. Bradshaw was his handler.

"That's right," Bradshaw said. "Not always. It's less likely in urban areas. But it's not too busy here on Lantern Beach yet. The ventilation system inside cars actually leave a trail that well-trained dogs can sniff out."

"That would come in really handy right now."

"I'll see if Dillinger can take over here, and I'll go get Ranger," Bradshaw said.

Ty thanked him and gave him his coordinates. He then began pacing the area, trying to figure out exactly where the car disappeared to.

As he did, Colton's hand clamped over his shoulder. "We're going to find her."

Ty nodded, but that didn't relieve the tightness in his chest.

Whoever was behind this was playing a deadly game. And apparently, this other person was holding all the right cards.

Annabeth was missing.

Cassidy had been taken.

Three people had died in the past few days.

And evidence had been planted making his wife look guilty.

Ten minutes later, Bradshaw arrived with Ranger in tow. At the urging of Colton, Ty had slipped back into the Blackout headquarters and grabbed a shirt that Cassidy wore yesterday. He placed it in a bag, and now he let Ranger sniff inside it.

The dog's nose went to the ground, and he began walking. They followed behind him, moving as fast as they could while the dog was fresh on the scent.

Ty knew he had no time to waste. Every minute that ticked past was one minute further he got from Cassidy.

One minute closer to death she might become.

Nothing about that thought was okay.

CHAPTER TWENTY-NINE

FRANTICALLY, Cassidy felt around the trunk. There had to be a way out. She just needed to find it.

Kicking out the taillight would no longer help her. The only thing it would have done earlier was to allow her to see where she was. And, ultimately, even kicking it out a little had let water get into the vehicle more quickly.

The water rose to her elbows.

The car must be on an angle. Cassidy assumed the driver had pushed the vehicle into the sound. The ocean would have more waves, more movement.

The Pamlico Sound, in most areas, wasn't that deep. That meant they'd probably gone to some type of boat launch area. It was the only thing that made sense.

But nobody would ever see the car in the water. They wouldn't know where to find her.

No, Cassidy couldn't think like that. She just needed to concentrate on getting out of here. Somehow.

Cassidy had already felt around the perimeter of the trunk uncountable times. There was nothing. The back of the sedan had been cleared, and there wasn't even a spare tire. There were no latches or triggers or any way to release this trunk from where she was.

She suppressed a cry and tried to feel around again.

It had been dark earlier, but now the darkness felt deeper. There was no way to see any light.

Instead, cool water continued to trickle around her. Considering the fact it was trickling, it rose surprisingly quickly.

She couldn't die like this.

More panic threatened to consume her. *Think, Cassidy. Think.*

But no viable ideas came to mind. There was no way she could claw her way out of this. Or kick her way out. Or scream until someone heard her.

The car was like a coffin and the water around her the dirt.

Suddenly, her skin felt like it was nearly crawling off of her. Her lungs tightened.

If the water continued to come in at this rate, she wouldn't have much time. Maybe five minutes, if she estimated correctly. Once the water filled the trunk, she might be able to hold her breath a couple of minutes. Maybe.

But that still didn't help her.

If she couldn't get out of here, then her struggle right now was no use.

She kicked the backseat one more time.

Nothing happened.

At that realization, despair began to creep in.

RANGER WAS hot on the trail of something.

Thank goodness.

Ty and Colton ran behind the dog—and Bradshaw. The two were a team.

They moved as fast as they could.

Ranger had taken them out on the highway that cut through the island. He headed south, away from the Blackout complex and down closer to the resort and residential area.

The dog had probably already gone a mile and didn't seem to be slowing down.

How much farther would they need to go?

All the way to the other end of the island? Because if that was the case, it would take them a long time to get there.

Ty only hoped when they found Cassidy that she was okay.

Please, Lord. Please.

A new sound filled his ears. A car was coming behind him, he realized.

Ty turned and waved, trying to signal for the car to slow down.

But when he saw who was behind the wheel, he scowled.

Watkins.

That man was the last person that he wanted to see right now.

Watkins pulled up beside him. "What's going on?"

"Just a training exercise." Ty didn't slow his steps and continued to jog behind Ranger.

"Is it? Isn't it interesting that you'd do it now of all times? Speaking of which, have you seen your wife? I had a few more questions for her."

"Last I heard, she was tied up with something

concerning the island. But I don't know. She doesn't answer to me."

Watkins glared at him. "Maybe you should keep your woman more under control."

"Cassidy isn't the type of woman you can control, and that's exactly what I like about her."

Watkins continued to glower. "Well, if you see her, tell her I want to talk to her."

"Will do." Ty watched as the man slowly pulled away.

Then he turned back to the crew in front of him.

Ranger sprinted another quarter mile before turning and heading down a gravel road.

Ty narrowed his eyes. He'd been down here before.

A small harbor waited at the end of this lane, and some houseboats were docked in the area. In fact, this was where Ty and Cassidy had ended up finding the Shacklefords.

Had somebody taken Cassidy to one of those houseboats?

Ty didn't know. And it didn't matter right now. All that mattered was finding his wife.

As they reached the end of the lane, the Pamlico Sound came into view. Ranger stopped right where the water met the sand.

Ty looked down and saw tire tracks heading into the water.

Had someone backed a boat into the water there? Had they put Cassidy onboard, just like they'd done with Annabeth?

He scanned the horizon but saw nothing.

Whoever had been here had already gotten away.

So how was Ty going to find Cassidy now?

CHAPTER THIRTY

THE WATER REACHED Cassidy's chin. In another minute or two, it would completely cover her face.

Cassidy angled her mouth so her lips reached the highest point of the trunk—the last place that should be filled.

Even though the water was probably sixty-five degrees, it felt freezing. Her hands were going numb. Or maybe it was the fear that made her body feel like this. She wasn't sure.

As she pressed her face into the metal, Cassidy prayed that Ty knew how much she loved him. That Annabeth would be found. That the girl was safe.

She hoped her friends knew how healing they'd been on her journey of moving here and settling in with her new identity. Their times together had meant the world to her.

The volleyball games on the beach. The bonfires at sunset. The Bible studies. The times they'd shared their lives over a meal.

Lisa and Braden. Skye and Austin. Wes and Paige. Pastor Jack and Juliette. Mac.

Cassidy couldn't forget Mac. The man had become one of her favorite people in the world.

It was hard to believe that she might not ever see any of them again.

She didn't want to give up.

She didn't think that was what she was doing.

But there was just no way she could get out of this trunk on her own.

These people . . . they'd wanted to frame her for Samuel's death. Now that they'd successfully done that, they wanted her to suffer. To die slowly.

The water lapped at her lips. As she opened her mouth to take a breath, some seeped inside. Desperation wanted to claw at her chest. At the same time, a strange sense of peace filled her.

If she was going to go, at least she knew she was right with God.

Still, she pressed her face into the metal above her.

The last thing Cassidy remembered thinking before the water completely covered her was how much she loved Ty.

———

"WHAT'S OUR NEXT MOVE?" Colton asked.

Ty put his hands on his hips as he glanced around the old harbor area. What were they missing? Should they check the houseboats?

But if Cassidy was there, Ranger would have led them in that direction.

Instead, Ranger remained firmly planted at the edge of the water.

Like he might do if Cassidy had been driven off in a boat.

"I don't know," Ty finally said.

Just then, Ranger stood at attention and began barking at the water.

"What is he doing?" Ty glanced at Bradshaw.

Bradshaw's brow furrowed as he shrugged. "I'm not sure."

"It's almost like he senses something we don't . . ." Colton said.

"You're right. It is." Ty's jaw twitched. What were they missing?

Bradshaw pointed to the water. "Can you see those bubbles coming out of the water there?"

Ty narrowed his eyes as he looked closer.

Bradshaw was right.

There *were* bubbles coming out of the water.

"Something's down there . . ." Ty muttered.

Without saying anything else, Ty and Colton rushed toward the water. Ty quickly emptied his pockets, leaving everything on shore. He didn't want anything to slow him down.

As soon as they were deep enough, Colton and Ty dove into the Pamlico and swam out to where the bubbles had surfaced.

Ty ducked under the water and opened his eyes.

It was a car.

Under the water.

The question was, was Cassidy inside?

CHAPTER THIRTY-ONE

WORKING QUICKLY, Ty opened the back door.

Cassidy wasn't inside the car.

But she might be in the trunk.

But how would he get inside without a crowbar? The car was an older model, too old to have a trunk release lever on the driver's side.

Still holding his breath, he climbed into the backseat. Colton followed his lead and climbed into the car from the other side.

Together, they grabbed the backseat. Using all their strength, they tugged on it.

Nothing.

They tugged again.

Again, nothing.

Ty was running out of air. He'd need to surface again.

But that extra time could mean life or death.

With a nod to each other, they pulled at the seat one more time.

This time, it gave.

As it did, something floated from the dark recesses of the trunk.

Cassidy.

And she was unconscious.

But not dead. She couldn't be dead.

Please, Lord, don't let her be dead.

Ty wrapped his arm around her chest and pulled her from the car. He surfaced and drew in a deep breath. Carefully, he placed Cassidy's head on his chest and began swimming back to the shore.

As soon as their feet hit dry land, Colton helped carry Cassidy onto the sand.

Ty put his finger to her neck.

She still had a pulse, but it was faint.

However, she wasn't conscious or breathing.

Ty tilted her head back and began rescue breathing.

Please, Lord. Let this work!

He continued pushing air into her lungs.

Again.

And again.

"Come on, Cassidy . . . breathe!" Ty muttered. "Breathe!"

He pushed more air in.

More.

More.

"Cassidy, please . . ." His voice cracked as he stared at her lifeless figure.

At his words, Cassidy's eyes flung open.

She coughed, water leaving her lungs.

Ty turned her and patted her back, trying to clear her lungs.

Finally, she drew in a long, labored breath.

She froze a moment as if gathering herself.

Gasping in another breath, she shot up.

Her eyes were wide and almost crazed as she looked around.

Then her gaze fell on Ty.

Her body seemed to go limp at the sight of him.

In one motion, Ty pulled her in his arms and held her.

Cassidy clung to him, her arms circling his neck.

"I'm alive." Her voice sounded raw with emotion . . . and surprise.

Her stark words made it clear that she hadn't expected to survive this.

"You found me," she whispered.

"Of course we did." Ty kissed the top of her head. "Ranger was a huge help."

"I'll have to buy him a big ham bone later."

"Are you okay?" Ty pulled away just enough to see her face. He had no idea what had transpired in the time since she had been snatched.

Cassidy nodded, but she still didn't look like herself. She was obviously rattled.

"We have to find these guys," she said.

"I know."

Someone had tried to kill her. But why try to kill her now? These people had opportunities before. It seemed strange that they would do this now.

"Maybe we should have Doc Clemson check you out." Worry clutched Ty's chest as he stared at Cassidy's pale face.

He'd never forget the horror of those few minutes in the car.

Cassidy had almost died.

He would do anything to protect her.

Cassidy shook her head in response to his statement about going to see the doctor. "We don't have time. Not now. We have other more important matters to attend to."

CASSIDY DREW IN A DEEP BREATH, still trying to gather her bearings.

Everything that had happened still seemed surreal. But she didn't have the luxury of recovering.

She simply needed to keep breathing.

Cassidy tried to push herself to her feet, but she was weaker than she'd thought.

Ty stood and then helped her stand. But her knees still felt wobbly.

Facing death had that effect on people.

"What exactly happened?" Ty still held onto her elbow as if afraid she might fall.

Cassidy explained the threat she'd received before being abducted. Looking back, maybe she could have done something differently. But it was too late for that.

"I knew I shouldn't go alone, but you were preoccupied with Gail," she said. "I had to make a split-second decision."

"Somebody probably wanted to get you out there alone." Ty scowled. "They may have even known about everything else going on and banked on the fact you wouldn't have backup."

"I'm guessing that they did."

"So you're saying that whoever is involved with this might also be involved with this investigation?" Bradshaw's voice hardened at the possibility.

"I don't know." Cassidy pushed some wet strands of hair away from her face. "As much as I keep trying to put these pieces together, I haven't been successful yet. Are there any updates I need to know about?"

"I left Dillinger to finish securing the crime scene at the salt pond and to make sure the body was transported to the morgue," Bradshaw said. "We'll continue with the investigation, of course. But I feel like Dillinger and I were thorough."

"And what's going on with Gail?" Cassidy asked Ty.

"I let Rocco entertain her for a while."

Cassidy raised her eyebrows. "Good call. She'll be very distracted by his accent."

"I know he can hold her off for a while, but I don't know how long. Then we're going to have to figure out what to tell her."

Cassidy shivered and wrapped her arms over her chest.

"I wish I had something to offer you," Ty said. "A jacket or a blanket."

"It's okay. I am just thankful to be alive. I'm so

thankful for all of you. I don't know how I'll ever repay you."

"Repay us by clearing your name and becoming police chief again," Bradshaw said.

She thought about his words a moment before nodding. "I'll do my best."

Just then, Ty's cell phone rang. Ty picked it from the ground where he'd left it and stared at the screen. "It's Paige. Do you want me to answer?"

Cassidy nodded. "Maybe she has an update."

Ty put the phone on speaker and held it out so everyone could hear. "Hey, Paige, what's going on?"

"I just overheard something as I was passing the conference room." Paige's voice sounded just above a whisper.

Cassidy stepped closer. "Paige . . . are you okay?"

"Cassidy! I tried your phone, but you didn't answer."

"I was . . . indisposed for a few minutes." Cassidy frowned, shoving down the bad memories. "What's going on? Why are you whispering?"

"I'm in the supply closet. I've been trying to listen to everything going on in the conference room. I know there are things I'm not supposed to hear."

"In other words, you're eavesdropping on the FBI and don't want them to find out," Cassidy clarified.

"Exactly," Paige said. "And I just heard Special Agent Watkins say that he got an arrest warrant . . . for you. He's coming to find you now. I wanted to let you know."

Cassidy's heart thumped into her chest. "Thanks, Paige. I really appreciate you letting me know."

As Ty ended the call and put the phone away, they all looked at each other.

"We ran into Watkins on our way over here. He knows I'm out this way. If he's armed with an arrest warrant, he might decide to hound me again for more information," Ty said. "It's not safe for you to be here, Cassidy."

Cassidy had to figure out what she was going to do, and she didn't have much time to make her decision.

CHAPTER THIRTY-TWO

CASSIDY'S MIND RACED.

Whatever she decided could change the course of her future. Not just *her* future, but also the future of those around her. The fact burdened her.

"Cassidy?"

She looked up and saw Ty staring at her. His blue eyes searched her, almost like he could see into her soul. She'd never had a connection like this until she'd met Ty. When she'd realized how much she loved him, she'd known at that moment that the two of them were practically made for each other. Before, she'd thought the very notion was just a childhood fantasy.

She drew in a deep breath, knowing she couldn't

put this off any longer. "If I'm arrested, I won't be able to find Annabeth. I won't be able to help her."

Ty tilted his head as if trying to read between the lines. "So what do you want to do?"

She licked her lips before blurting, "I need to run."

Ty blinked and jerked his head back with surprise. "Run? Where would you go?"

"I don't know. I just need to disappear for a while."

"Are you sure this is what you want to do?" Ty's voice sounded painfully quiet as his question hung in the air.

Was she sure? Not really. But given the two options, this one seemed the best.

Whatever the outcome, she'd have to face the consequences. She'd been backed into a corner.

"I can't tell you where I'm going to be or any other details," she finally said. "I don't want to put any of you in a bad position when Watkins comes and asks—and he will come asking questions."

Ty's jaw hardened. He said nothing for a minute until finally nodding. "I understand. But you have to be careful. Not only do you have a potential killer after you but also the FBI. I can't be close to protect you."

"I know." She stepped closer. "I'll be careful. I promise. I just need your gun."

Ty pulled it from his holster and handed it to her. Then he grabbed something from his pocket. "Take my burner. I know the number, and I'll buy a new one so we can be in touch. I'll text you that number."

"Thank you."

"I also put a tracking app on it just in case."

"Smart thinking."

Cassidy reached up on her tiptoes and her lips met Ty's in a lingering kiss. When she pulled away, she stared into his gaze, hoping to express exactly how she felt.

"I don't know what's going to happen, but just know that I love you." Her throat burned as she said the words.

The intensity in Ty's eyes made her heart ache.

"I love you too, Cassidy." His voice cracked.

She stepped back and nodded at Bradshaw and Colton. Then she darted into the woods. She needed to disappear. But first, she needed some clothes. Maybe even a car.

And she didn't have much time to figure it all out.

THE LAST HOUR had been a flurry of activity. Ty had called Rocco and asked him to let Gail know that an emergency had come up and Ty and Cassidy wouldn't be able to make it back.

Rocco said he'd do his best to talk Gail through the situation.

Ty knew if anybody could do it, Rocco could.

Bradshaw and Dillinger were working on the car found in the Pamlico. That's what they were saying about the situation. That nobody had been found inside. Bradshaw didn't even tell Dillinger that fact.

Ty hated to keep the information from his friends, but the fewer people who knew, the fewer people who'd be tempted to lie to protect Cassidy. He didn't want to put anyone in an unfair position.

They had the vehicle towed, and Ty was hoping forensics might turn up some information from the car itself. But knowing what he did about the people behind these crimes, he realized it was doubtful.

As Ty stood there observing the officers work, two black SUVs pulled onto the scene.

He knew what was about to happen next and braced himself.

Watkins had arrived.

The man climbed from the car, sunglasses on and that arrogant demeanor surrounding him as he strode toward them.

"What's going on here?" he demanded as if knowing was his right.

Ty didn't say anything. He was just here as a civilian, and it wasn't his place. In theory, at least.

Instead, Bradshaw stepped forward. "We were patrolling the area and noticed a car had been submerged in the water. We had it towed out so we could investigate."

Watkins' eyebrows flickered as if he were a human lie detector. "Anything suspicious inside?"

"Not that we've found so far." Bradshaw kept his voice professional. "But given everything that's happened on the island, we want to be sure."

"If you do find anything, I expect to know what it is."

"Of course." Bradshaw nodded coolly, not showing any signs of deception.

Then Watkins turned toward Ty. "Why are you wet?"

"Colton and I checked out the car to make sure no one was inside."

"Was there?"

"No sir."

Watkins' pressed his lips together. "Where's your wife?"

Ty didn't bother to straighten or show the man any special favor. He remained where he was, standing near Dillinger's car with his arms crossed. "I don't know. Like I said earlier, she doesn't have to tell me her every move. Why?"

"Because I have a warrant for her arrest."

Ty swallowed hard and widened his eyes, careful to show surprise. "A warrant for her arrest? Why do you want to arrest Cassidy?"

"She was the last person known to be with Stephens. We believe she lured him to Lantern Beach under the guise of talking and then killed him in the woods." His hardened voice sounded so confident, so sure.

"What would her motive be?"

"To cover something up," Watkins said. "We're still trying to figure out what."

Ty loosened his arms and shrugged, determined not to give Watkins the satisfaction of seeing any fear or doubt. "Sounds circumstantial to me. You know Cassidy isn't a part of this. She isn't a killer."

The man's eyebrows flickered again. "The evidence begs to differ."

"The evidence can be misinterpreted. Cassidy

would sacrifice herself before hurting somebody. You've got this all wrong." Ty's voice held a matching confidence. No one would ever convince him his wife was guilty. No one.

"We also found the murder weapon," Watkins said.

Ty tried to keep his expression placid even as surprise burst inside him. "Did you?"

"It was in an old bunker near the Blackout property."

"Is that right? How did you manage to find that?"

"We got a tip. We have a search warrant, and we'll be combing through your home to see if the knife came from there."

Ty would bet anything that the man who'd been posing as their maintenance worker had secretly been spying on him—had maybe even followed him. Someone would have to be skilled to do that without Ty's knowledge, but he supposed it was possible.

Ty kept his voice even as he said, "Cassidy would be too smart for that. If you discover it is, it's because someone set her up."

"I'll be the judge of that." Watkins bristled even more. "Now, where can I find Chief Chambers?"

"I have no idea. She didn't tell me where she was

going. I'm guessing you checked the Blackout facility?"

"No one there has seen her either."

Ty shrugged, keeping his voice nonchalant. "Then maybe she's working a case."

Watkins pulled his sunglasses down just enough for Ty to see his scowl. "Then I'll be looking for her."

Ty offered a stiff nod. "May justice prevail."

As the man walked away, Ty softened his shoulders. He prayed that Cassidy was able to find somewhere safe to lie low for a while.

He knew she was competent. But these circumstances could test even the most seasoned law enforcement officer.

CHAPTER THIRTY-THREE

CASSIDY CUT THROUGH THE WOODS, across lanes, behind cottages, and through more woods. Finally, she paused by a house.

She didn't want to get anybody else involved with this.

But some things couldn't be avoided.

This was one of them.

She checked to make sure no one was looking before dashing from the trees to the back door.

A moment later, Skye Brooks appeared. Her friend, with her long, dark hair and hippy clothing style, stared at her. A knot formed between Skye's eyes as she slid open the patio door.

"Cassidy?" Skye nearly gawked. "What's going on? You look . . . terrible."

Cassidy didn't argue with that assessment. She knew her hair was still wet, along with her clothes. No doubt she'd gotten dirty as she ran through the woods. The stress of the situation had her gasping in deep breaths.

"It's a long story. I can't tell you the details. I'm sorry."

"I understand." Skye stepped back, that knot still on her forehead. "What do you need?"

"A change of clothes. Maybe a hat and some sunglasses. And I need to know if you still have that old car Austin used to drive."

"Yeah, it's parked on the side of the house."

"Does it work?"

Skye shrugged. "Most of the time."

"Is there any way I could borrow it?"

"You're scaring me, Cassidy." Skye's voice sounded as if she was still in shock as she processed this turn of events.

"I'm sorry. I'd tell you the details if I could. But believe me, I don't want to put you in that position. It's for your own good."

Skye stared at her another moment before coming out of her shock and quickly nodding. "Of course. Let me go grab some things for you. If you want to clean up in the bathroom, I'll bring them to you."

Twenty minutes later, Cassidy had tied her hair back into a loose ponytail. She'd pulled on a black baseball cap, and she held aviator glasses in her hands. Meanwhile, Skye had let her borrow some black jeans and a sweatshirt along with some dry tennis shoes.

The disguise wouldn't trick everybody. Not by any means. But at least Cassidy wouldn't stand out. That was the important thing.

She folded her wet clothes and tucked them under her arm. She couldn't risk leaving them here in case Watkins came to look for her. She didn't want any evidence to be left behind.

As she lifted the wet police uniform into her arms, something fell to the floor. She reached down and picked up a wooden ice cream cone that Ty had carved for her when they'd first met.

As she stared at it, her heart lurched into her throat.

When she'd first come to this area, Cassidy had disguised herself as an ice cream lady, and she'd driven an old truck all around the island to sell her sugary, cold treats. She hadn't realized when she started, but the act had almost been her way of patrolling the streets just as she had done when she started out as a rookie cop.

She'd been unable to look the other way when she saw things that shouldn't be happening. Even though she was supposed to hide her real identity, she couldn't stop herself from fighting for justice.

It was just a part of her being.

And Ty had fit into that picture beautifully. He'd been the best thing she could have ever asked for.

She brought the ice cream cone to her lips and kissed it.

Part of her felt like she was saying goodbye to this life.

Tears heated her eyes.

She couldn't bear that thought.

She sucked in a quick breath. She couldn't think like this now.

Too much was on the line.

Quickly, she slipped the wooden ice cream cone into her pocket. She carried it with her all the time, calling it her good luck charm.

She could use some of that now.

As Cassidy stepped out from the bathroom and found her friend again, Skye pulled her into a hug.

"I'm scared for you," she whispered.

"There are just some things that I have to do." As

Cassidy said the words, she had to wonder if this was the last time she'd ever see her friend.

She didn't want to think that way.

But she had no choice except to face the truth.

Realistically speaking, Cassidy's life might not ever be the same again. She might not be able to go back to her oceanfront cottage and live the rest of her happy little life there with Ty and Kujo. Not if Watkins had his way. And not if the ones responsible for these crimes had theirs either.

"I will see you again, right?"

Cassidy paused. She wanted to say yes. But the words wouldn't leave her lips.

Instead, she squeezed her friend's hand. "Thank you for everything. Every time I wear that jacket you gave me when I first arrived and we were walking down by the pier, I think of you and your kindness to me. You were my first real friend when I came here."

"Cassidy..."

Before any tears could flow from her eyes, Cassidy headed out the door.

She had no time to waste.

BRADSHAW and the gang hadn't found anything of note in the car, which had been stolen from Raleigh two days earlier.

The news didn't surprise Ty.

Knowing there was nothing else he would get from that scene, he headed back to Blackout. His mind was on Cassidy, though.

Where was she? Was she okay?

And what about Annabeth? He needed to find the girl. Too much time had passed.

Ty found Rocco in the lobby—alone. Perfect. Ty really needed an update from his friend.

"Hey." Rocco stood from where he'd been reading a book near the fireplace. "I was hoping to catch you. Gail left about thirty minutes ago."

"What did she say?"

"That she's going to come back in two days."

A moment of relief filled Ty. "Did she seem concerned?"

Rocco shrugged, his hands resting in his pockets. "I fibbed a little and told her that you two were planning a princess photo shoot on the beach for Annabeth. That seemed to appease her."

"That's good news." But Ty's relief was replaced with a surge of apprehension. "But I don't feel great about all this. Not at all."

"I don't know what's going on, but whatever you need me to do, let me know."

"Will do." Ty started toward the office area. "Thank you for everything you've already done."

Ty couldn't stop thinking about how close Cassidy had come to death. His lungs tightened until he could hardly breathe each time he remembered being underwater and trying to get her free from that car.

It had been so close. So close.

As he sat behind his desk, his thoughts went to Annabeth. Where was she? And how could he find her?

The kidnappers said to wait for instructions. But when Cassidy had been given those instructions, it had only been a setup to try to kill her.

He wished that all this made sense, but it didn't. And he needed to figure out exactly what his next step should be.

He was going to examine every aspect of this case again, starting from the very beginning when he and Cassidy found Annabeth on the beach near their cottage.

Somewhere in the details lay answers.

He just had to figure out which details to focus on.

CHAPTER THIRTY-FOUR

CASSIDY NEEDED TO USE A COMPUTER.

Yet she couldn't be spotted.

Her mind raced through the possibilities of where she might go before stopping at one place.

Feeling a touch of nerves, she drove Skye and Austin's old sedan down the road toward her destination. She knew that after a certain amount of time, Watkins would probably get desperate. He might put up roadblocks to find her. He'd search people going on and off the island via the ferry system. He'd do whatever was necessary to find her.

But right now, Watkins most likely thought Cassidy was just on a job somewhere.

That meant she maybe had only another hour or two before he got suspicious.

She needed to act fast. Killing an FBI agent was a serious offense. The Bureau would put all their manpower into finding the person responsible. If they thought that person was Cassidy, then she was a dead woman walking right now.

Her throat squeezed as she swallowed, and her heart continued to pound out of control. One slipup, and this could all be over. That's why she couldn't allow herself to make any mistakes.

Finally, she pulled down a secluded lane leading to a rental house named *Shore Enough*. The property was surrounded by trees with only a small canal as its neighbor.

Cassidy had been called out to this place a few weeks ago when the owner had been in town reno-vating the interior. The woman thought someone had broken in. It turned out to be her grandson who'd stopped by for a surprise visit. He'd triggered the security system in the process.

The woman—Norma Segal—had casually mentioned that the first renters of the season weren't coming until Memorial Day weekend. She gave Cassidy a code to get inside and had asked her to keep an eye on the place if she could.

Cassidy didn't normally keep an eye on private

vacation rentals for people while they were out of town—at least, she didn't focus on one house over another.

But, right now, this code could come in handy.

Cassidy pulled her car to the edge of the woods, where nobody driving past would see it. She had to think through every move, every possibility for being caught.

Moving quickly, she climbed the stairs and punched in the code at the front door.

As she did, she looked up. Norma had security cameras here. For that reason, Cassidy couldn't act suspicious. She needed to look like she was simply the police chief coming to do her good deed.

But as she grabbed the door handle, a voice sounded above her.

"Chief Chambers? Is that you?"

Cassidy's heart pounded harder. This security system allowed owners to talk to anybody outside their house.

Cassidy knew she needed to play it cool. She glanced up at the camera and smiled. "I promised you I'd stop by and check on things. So here I am."

"Must be your day off. You're not in uniform."

"It's true." She glanced down at her outfit. "I'm

trying to catch up on a few things, but I just happened to be coming by here so I thought I'd stay true to my word."

"I appreciate it. Feel free to grab some water for yourself while you're in there. Oh, and can you check that the fridge is still working? I keep having power outages at my place for some reason."

"Will do." But Cassidy knew what that meant.

If Norma knew when Cassidy had come, she would also know when Cassidy left. That meant that Cassidy might have to get creative here—or that she didn't have much time.

It was just one more complication to an already complicated situation.

Once inside, Cassidy quickly rushed to a desk located on the first level. She remembered seeing it when she was here before.

She turned on the computer and grabbed the laminated piece of paper beside the desktop.

Quickly, she punched in the password that had been left for renters.

She needed to do a quick internet search.

She had no time to waste.

AS TY SAT at his desk, he researched the cable company that had supposedly sent someone out to his house.

Just as he'd thought, the company hadn't sent anyone. They'd said the service call was canceled.

One of the bad guys had been in his house, and Ty hadn't known.

The man had been good. Really good. Ty generally had good instincts, but this guy had slipped past.

His phone rang, and Ty saw it was his friend Wes O'Neill.

Though he didn't feel like chatting, his friend usually only called if he had a reason.

Ty quickly hit Talk. "Hey, man."

"Ty, what's going on? The FBI showed up here at the beach right before I was going out for a kayak tour. They asked me if I'd seen Cassidy."

Great. The feds were already searching all over the island. Ty shouldn't be surprised.

"I can't tell you any details." Ty clicked on his pen as his thoughts raced. "But she didn't do anything wrong. She's being framed."

"Man. I'm sorry to hear that. What should I do?"

"Just tell the truth. You don't know where she is, right?"

"Right. I've wanted to catch up with you guys for a while now, but this wasn't the way I wanted to do it."

"I appreciate your concern. I'll let you know if I need anything."

Ty had been blessed, he realized as he ended the call. He had so many good friends who'd do anything to help him. He appreciated that fact more than he'd ever expressed.

Ty clicked his pen again before finally putting it down, driving himself crazy with the nervous tick.

He'd been reviewing the details of the case for the past hour.

But nothing really jumped out at him.

His mind kept going back to the Shacklefords.

He'd bet they knew something about what was happening here and could offer some type of answers.

He was also bothered by the fact that Alexandria Manchester had been transferred to a CIA facility. There was something fishy about that entire situation.

Only a few moments after Ty hung up with Wes, his phone rang again.

His heartbeat quickened when he saw it was his

friend from the FBI, Harry Overton. He quickly answered, hoping Harry had some type of update for him.

"Sorry it took me a little bit longer than I expected," Harry said. "But I was doing some digging into Watkins and his background, trying to keep everything on the down low so no one got suspicious."

"I appreciate that. Did you find out anything?" Hope tried to rise in Ty, but he pushed it down. There was no need to get excited. Not yet.

"I know this isn't what you want to hear. But I couldn't find anything. Watkins can be a real pain sometimes, but he appears to do good work."

Ty silently groaned. That *definitely* wasn't what he expected to hear. If his friend's words were true, then why had Samuel warned Cassidy not to trust Watkins? He had to have a reason for it.

"You didn't discover anything else?" Ty asked in a last-ditch effort for information.

"No, I'm sorry. I didn't. I know he's there on your island right now, investigating the death of Special Agent Samuel Stephens. I don't know if that has something to do with this or not."

"It's probably better if I don't tell you."

"From everything I heard, Stephens was a good

agent too. I don't know what's going on in Lantern Beach, but I'll be praying that everything works out."

"Thanks. I appreciate that."

Ty chatted with his friend about Watkins for a few more minutes. But as Ty ended the call, he didn't have any more answers than he did before.

CHAPTER THIRTY-FIVE

CASSIDY STARED at the computer and the information she'd pulled up on the screen.

A picture stared back at her.

A picture of a man who was in his fifties with salt-and-pepper hair, a Roman nose, and intelligent brown eyes.

There had only been one person she could think of that all these crimes could lead back to. Someone powerful. Someone smart. Someone with a lot on the line.

Gerald Mecklenburg, the assistant CIA director.

It had to be him.

She stared at his picture. At his long list of accolades. At the moments that had distinguished his career.

But the man was too smart and too powerful to come to this island and act out any of his criminal endeavors himself. He had people secretly working for him. It was the only thing that made sense.

The question was, who? Was this person lurking in the shadows? Or was this person—these people—hiding in plain sight? Maybe it was even somebody with connections.

After all, someone like Mecklenburg would have uncountable people at his disposal. Had he blackmailed somebody into doing his dirty work? Paid off somebody?

She had a feeling the man who'd pretended to be Ronnie Baskins had been hired help—that was based on his taunting attitude. Someone who was being blackmailed would have capitulated more.

She turned back to the computer, trying to find any type of connection she could between Mecklenburg and anyone here on Lantern Beach.

But Cassidy found nothing. The only thing Cassidy could assume was that maybe Mecklenburg had one of the FBI agents working here on the island in his pocket.

She remembered Rohl.

The agent was a rookie, and his gaze wasn't

always steady. Was that because he was hiding something?

She nibbled on her bottom lip as the questions raced through her mind. It was going to be hard to get to the bottom of this on her own.

Using the rental house phone, she called Ty's cell, praying he'd answer the unknown number. She wanted to save her battery for as long as she could since she didn't have a charger with her.

On the second ring, Ty's voice came on the line.

"It's Cassidy," she rushed. "I'm okay. But I'm not going to tell you where I am."

"Cassidy . . . it's good to hear your voice. I'm glad you called."

The way he said the words made her realize there had been a development. "Did something happen?"

He updated her on his call with his FBI friend.

Cassidy shook her head and leaned back in her seat, trying to let his words make sense. But they didn't, no matter how she looked at them.

"So this guy really thinks Watkins is decent?" She found that hard to believe. Samuel wasn't sure he could trust him. Why should Cassidy?

"That's what Harry said. He said the man could be a pain, but that he did things by the book. That he didn't put a lot of emotion into his investigations, but he stuck with the facts. I have to say that from everything I've observed that's probably true."

"That actually ties in with what I needed to ask you about." Cassidy stared at the man's picture on the computer screen. "I'm convinced that Gerald Mecklenburg is behind this and that he may have one of the FBI agents working here in his pocket."

"What?"

"Think about it. He has the resources to frame people. To cover up crimes. To transfer Alexandria Manchester somewhere without anyone knowing."

"Good points."

"I don't have the time or the opportunity to look into all the FBI agents' backgrounds myself. I can't stay anywhere for too long. Could you check them out?"

"I can do that. But what I really want to do is to be out there searching for Annabeth." Regret whispered through his tone.

"This is the best thing you can do to help me right now," Cassidy said. "And text me your new phone number so I can call it from my burner phone. There's no telling if somebody could be tracing your calls as well."

"I'll do that."

"That said, we should be getting off soon." She paused, feeling a change in the air. After this week, would their lives ever be the same again? Her gut told her no. "I love you, Ty."

"I love you too." Ty's voice sounded strained as he said the words.

Just as Cassidy put the phone back onto the receiver, she heard a creak.

Had that come from outside on the deck? Was someone here?

Her lungs froze at the thought.

Quietly, she turned the computer off and slipped into a bedroom down the hallway.

As she pressed herself behind the door, she drew her gun.

She had to be prepared for whatever was about to happen next.

But at any minute, she expected to see the FBI invade the house and arrest her.

TY DID his best to look up all the information on the FBI agents who had come to the island. He couldn't remember all the first and last names, however. Most of them had only introduced them-selves by their last names.

Finally, he looked away from the computer and rubbed the skin between his eyes. Soon, it would be getting dark, and that would present a whole new set of challenges—as well as offering cover.

But Ty knew what Cassidy was saying. It seemed like whoever was behind this might have some type of inside connection.

This was getting him nowhere. While he believed in being prepared, right now what he wanted to do was to be out in the field. He wanted to be searching for Annabeth.

If only he had some clue as to where to go. If only he'd been allowed to tell people on the island that the girl was missing.

But Ty couldn't take that chance. It was risky. He knew that. But what else was he supposed to do?

He glanced at his cell as it beeped again.

A new message appeared.

His eyes widened as he read the words.

So sorry about your wife. But sometimes these things happen. Trust it's for the best.

Anger burned through his blood.

He quickly typed back.

Where is Annabeth?

No response.
He typed again.

What do you want?

Again, no response.

But then he immediately realized two things.

These people didn't know Cassidy was still alive. They thought she'd died when the car went into the water. Maybe he could use that fact to his advantage.

Also, if the FBI was involved, wouldn't they know that Cassidy was still alive? When they'd found Ty at the harbor, they would have realized something was going on, right?

He needed to think that through a little more.

Ty hoped that whoever was behind this paid dearly.

CHAPTER THIRTY-SIX

CASSIDY HEARD the footsteps outside on the deck. The next instant, she heard the door open. Heard someone walking across the floor. Heard something being slid.

As she glanced at the alarm clock on the night-stand, she saw the light flicker out. Had the power gone out again? What was going on? Why would someone cut the power right now? How would that help them?

She had no idea. Cassidy *did* know that Norma wouldn't be able to watch her come or go until power was restored. Maybe that could be a good thing.

Despite that, Cassidy remained behind the door. She gripped her gun, ready to act.

Until then, she listened.

She heard only one set of footsteps. She'd expected to hear many. Had expected that the FBI had somehow found her and were coming to capture her now.

The minutes ticked by as she waited.

Closing one eye, she peered out the crack of the door, trying to see something. Anything.

But it was getting dark, and the house was shaded already. With the power being out, everything was harder to see.

A moment later, the sound of someone whistling floated through the air.

Whistling? What sense did that make?

She needed to be patient. She couldn't play into someone's hands right now.

Footsteps pounded across the floor again. They were closer this time.

Cassidy tried to peer out again, tried to catch a glimpse of whatever was going on.

A man came into view.

She frowned.

He didn't look like an FBI agent.

In fact . . . he looked familiar. And he wore coveralls.

Cassidy squinted, trying to get a better look.

It was Merle Evans, she realized.

He was one of the maintenance men on the island. From what she could tell, it appeared he was about to change a light fixture.

She released her breath, holding back a laugh. This was no time to be humored.

But Cassidy was so relieved it was just Merle.

Still, she had other problems—like the fact she needed to get out of here without being seen so she could keep investigating.

CASSIDY PUT her sunglasses on and pulled her hat low as she drove down the road looking for any signs of trouble.

When Merle had disappeared for several minutes, probably to get some supplies from his truck, Cassidy had been able to sneak out of the house. She'd climbed into her car and had driven away, and she didn't think Merle had any clue.

And there was only one place that she could think to go.

The Lantern Beach harbor.

It was where all the avid fisherman and boatmen spent their time.

She'd already questioned several of them. But she wanted to see if anybody new was here.

If anyone had seen something suspicious happening on the water, it would be them. They knew these waterways like the back of their hands, as the saying went.

As Cassidy pulled into a parking space, her phone buzzed. The only person that could contact her on the burner was Ty.

She glanced down and saw his message.

They think you're dead.

Her heart pounded in her ears.

Apparently, these guys hadn't double-checked to make sure that putting her into the Pamlico Sound while in the trunk of the car had worked. They'd assume she'd died there in that watery grave.

A touch of satisfaction stretched through her. Maybe she could use that fact to her advantage.

But she didn't have time to do that right now.

At any moment, the FBI could track her down. She didn't want that to happen.

Her main concern right now was finding Anna-beth. As soon as the girl was located, then the FBI could do whatever they wanted with Cassidy. But she had to know that Annabeth was safe first.

As Cassidy climbed from her car, she reached into her pocket and felt that ice cream cone again. Her thoughts went to Ty.

She briefly closed her eyes and lifted a quick prayer.

Be with him now. Give him comfort. Help him to know that everything will be okay.

She released the cone back into her pocket and then began to stroll the docks. She didn't want any more people than necessary to see her. If they did, then when the FBI came around—because they would come around—those people would have to admit they'd seen Cassidy.

Most locals knew who she was. It would only be someone from out of town that might not recognize her.

She glanced around, looking for anybody she thought she might be able to talk to.

Then she heard a deep voice rumbling behind her. "If it isn't Cassidy Chambers. Long time no see."

CHAPTER THIRTY-SEVEN

"TY, there's somebody here to see you."

He looked up at Chloe Donovan, Blackout's administrative assistant, and narrowed his eyes.

"Special Agent Watkins is outside the gate." She frowned as if expecting Ty to react strongly. "What should I tell him?"

Ty was tempted to blow the man off. But he wasn't sure how much good that would do.

After another moment of thought, he finally nodded. "You can let him in."

Ty's mind raced as he waited for Watkins to appear. What was the man doing here? Was he coming to make more threats? Ty was about to find out.

A few minutes later, Watkins appeared in his doorway.

"Chambers," he said stiffly.

Ty didn't want to like this guy. He wanted to think that Watkins was somehow complicit in what was going on. But what if he was wrong? What if the man really was simply doing his job?

"What can I do for you?" Ty didn't bother to offer him a seat.

Watkins placed his hands on his hips as he stared Ty down. "I want you to shoot straight with me. Where is your wife? I've been looking all over the island, and no one has seen her."

"It's like I told you, she doesn't have to—"

"Tell you where she goes," Watkins finished with a hint of resentment in his voice. "I know. But that doesn't mean that you don't know where she is."

"I *don't* know where she is." Ty was thankful that Cassidy hadn't told him so he didn't have to lie right now.

Watkins' eyes narrowed. "I'm about five seconds away from arresting you as an accessory to murder."

Ty kept his expression level even as he felt emotions ramping up inside him. This guy wasn't playing. "What evidence do you have to prove that?"

"Cassidy *has* to have somebody helping her.

Maybe even somebody who hid that knife for her in that bunker. From what I've heard from the stories around town, you were held hostage down there once, weren't you?"

Ty continued to keep his expression even. "I'm not sure what that has to do with anything."

Watkins stepped closer, glaring down at Ty. "I'm about to shut down the entire island. More FBI agents are on the way. We're going to find your wife. Since she's considered armed and dangerous, my agents are permitted to shoot to kill."

Ty's gut tightened.

He had no doubt that Watkins meant his words.

Based on the way it sounded, they were all operating on borrowed time right now.

CASSIDY STARTED to reach for her gun as she turned around.

Her eyes widened when she spotted Jimmy James behind her. She flinched at the sight of him. "Jimmy? I didn't know you were back on the island."

The man reminded her of Brutus from the old Popeye cartoons. He was tall, muscular, and tough, with uncountable tattoos and a shaved head. Jimmy had a history of petty crimes on the island, but something about the man was still lovable. He'd helped Cassidy in the past, almost acting as an informant for a couple of cases.

Cassidy couldn't stop herself from liking him, despite his many failings.

"I didn't tell anybody I was coming back." Jimmy James placed his meaty hands on his hips and the fading sun highlighted the tattoo sleeves climbing up his arms. "I figured it was better that way."

"When did you get back?" Her shoulders tensed. Did he know that the FBI was looking for her? She didn't think he was the type to call the police on her but . . .

No slipups.

That had to be her goal right now.

He shrugged. "About three days ago. I've been keeping it low-key and staying in one of the boats down here that my friend owns."

An idea sparked inside her. Jimmy James was resourceful—and not always in a good way. But he was also observant and a great waterman.

Maybe . . .

She glanced up at him. "So you have a pretty good pulse on what's going on down here at the harbor, huh?"

"I'd like to think so." He shifted. "Why are you asking?"

"Some suspicious things have been happening on the water. But I'm having trouble tracking down any leads. Do you have any information that might help me?"

He stared at Cassidy a moment before glancing behind her. It was almost like he was checking to make sure no one was watching them—or to make sure none of his friends thought he was a snitch.

"No," he finally said. "Why would I know anything?"

Cassidy stepped closer and nudged Jimmy James behind a building, so that nobody would see them if they happened to pull up. She didn't want to take any chances.

"Look, it's important. It's really, really important. A little girl's life may depend on me having those answers."

"A little girl?"

Cassidy realized that if Jimmy James had been gone that long then he probably didn't know about Annabeth. It was better that he didn't know too many details.

"It's all hush-hush," she told him quietly, as if sharing a secret. "Let's just say that someone's life is in danger and that every minute matters. I believe this girl was taken from this island on a boat, but I need to figure out *where* she was taken. Any information that you might have . . ."

Jimmy James stared at Cassidy a moment, his mouth opening and shutting as if he were contemplating his actions.

Finally, Cassidy reached into her wallet and pulled out two twenties. She handed them to the man, knowing exactly how to speak his language. "Does this help you remember?"

His eyes lit with interest. "Money always helps. Might help with food and rent and getting back on my feet."

"If you offer me good information, I'll make sure to find more twenties with your name on them."

He nodded and glanced around again.

Cassidy's heart sped as she waited for what he had to say. She desperately prayed his information might lead to Annabeth.

CHAPTER THIRTY-EIGHT

TY HAD to make a split-second decision. He didn't want to trust Watkins. But if he wanted Cassidy to get out of the situation alive, maybe he needed to—at least, a little.

Ty swallowed hard before admitting, "There's more to the situation than you realize."

Watkins crossed his arms and continued to stare him down. "Why don't you share with me what that is?"

Ty remained silent a moment, still contemplating how much he should say.

Finally, he admitted, "She's being framed."

Watkins narrowed his eyes, clearly unimpressed. "You mentioned that."

"Maybe she's even being framed by one of the agents."

Watkins shook his head and let out a skeptical chuckle. "That's crazy. Why would one of my guys frame her?"

"Do you remember all the secrets that were being tossed about during that investigation into the Shacklefords?" Ty reminded him. "Secrets can have deadly consequences. And secrets can make people do things they otherwise wouldn't."

"Do you really think one of my guys is behind this? That they set her up? I think that's far-fetched."

"I know how it sounds," Ty said. "But I think somebody views Cassidy as too much of a threat."

Watkins remained silent a minute before finally shaking his head. "Why don't you tell me what else is going on?"

Ty pressed his lips together. Should he share more? Did he really have much of a choice at this point?

Cassidy's life was on the line. One of the agents could kill her in the name of justice.

Ty swallowed hard, knowing what he needed to do. However, he hoped the consequences were worth the payoff.

"Somebody snatched Annabeth and told us if we

involved any type of law enforcement that she would die," Ty kept his voice low. "Cassidy is out looking for her."

Watkins recoiled in surprise. "What? That's something that could've been mentioned sooner."

"We'll do anything we can to protect her."

"We need to put some people on this," Watkins said.

"If you're involved, they're going to kill her. I have no doubt they mean it. These guys have killed before, and they'll kill again."

Watkins frowned before letting out a long breath. "We'll come back to that subject in a minute. That still doesn't explain why your wife was with Samuel Stephens in the woods."

Ty prayed he wouldn't regret what he was about to say.

But if it meant saving Cassidy, then he had to tell the truth.

"Samuel Stephens put Cassidy in witness protection. That's why. He was her handler."

"THERE'S BEEN a lot of activity over on Duck Island," Jimmy James told her. "It's close to one of my favorite fishing holes, so I've been watching it."

"Duck Island? That place hasn't been used in years from what I've heard."

The island was between the Pamlico Sound and the mainland. Apparently, a hunting lodge had been built there nearly sixty years ago, but it had been mostly abandoned after the owner died.

The man's son had put a huge price tag on the property, and nobody wanted to pay the exorbitant amount. The whole place was run on solar panels and generators.

Apparently, it had been the place to be back in the day.

"Tell me what else you know," Cassidy said.

Jimmy James shrugged. "I've seen some people coming and going there. But it's been pretty low-key."

"If that opened up as a rental or if someone bought it, there would be talk all over the island."

"That's what I think too. Which makes me wonder what's going on there."

Cassidy had to get to that island. She wanted to see for herself what was going on there.

But first she had to figure out a way to travel there.

Her gaze met Jimmy James'. "Do you have access to a boat?"

"I might be able to get one. Why?" He tugged his ear and the gauge earring there.

"I'm going to need a ride over there. I'd like to check things out myself. I'll pay you."

His eyes lit. "I see. Give me a few minutes to see if I can find something for you."

"I'll do that. But Jimmy James, you can't tell anybody what you're doing or that you saw me. It's important."

He stared at her, questions in his gaze. But he didn't ask any of them.

"I understand, Chief. Whatever you need. Especially if a little girl's life is on the line here."

Gratitude filled her. But Cassidy would need help if that island was where Annabeth was being held.

And she needed to decide whether or not she was going to tell Ty what was going on.

CHAPTER THIRTY-NINE

AS CASSIDY SAT at the back of the skiff and glanced around, anticipation built in her.

If Annabeth was being held on Duck Island, how many people were there guarding her?

Cassidy would guess at least two—but maybe more.

If an FBI agent was in on this, he'd obviously have guys working for him. She wondered if Ty had found out anything.

She wanted to call him. She'd probably need backup. Someone besides Jimmy James.

But telling him would be a risk. She couldn't let Watkins catch wind of it.

She decided to wait and see what she found there. Then she'd let him know.

As the boat sped across the water, Cassidy kept her hat low, searching for any marine police or Coast Guard boats who might be on the lookout for her.

There was a really good possibility they were out there.

Just as the thought went through her head, she spotted a Coast Guard boat in the distance. She held her breath and ducked lower.

Maybe they were out doing something else.

But as the vessel turned toward them, she knew that wasn't the case.

"Jimmy James . . ."

She didn't have to say anything else. Jimmy James seemed to read her thoughts.

"There's a storage compartment beneath me," he said. "You're small. You can fit inside. If you go now, they won't see you."

She could hardly breathe. She wasn't used to being on this side of the law.

But she had little choice right now except to hide.

Moving quickly, she pulled the top from the storage compartment and climbed inside, squeezing between some old ropes that were stored there. The fit was snug, but at least the area was big enough to hold her.

As Jimmy James clamped the top down on her and she heard the latch click, she prayed that this wasn't a bad move.

A few minutes later, the skiff slowed then stopped. She heard Jimmy James call to someone. "What can I help you with?"

"Have you seen this woman?" a deep voice asked.

She imagined a Coast Guardsman showing Jimmy James her picture.

"That's Police Chief Chambers," Jimmy James said.

She squeezed her eyes shut, praying that she could trust Jimmy James. She thought she could. Yet she couldn't be 100 percent sure.

"Have you seen her in the past four or five hours?"

"I just got back into town," Jimmy James answered. "Decided I'd just go on a little joy ride to my favorite fishing hole. But I haven't seen the chief. Honestly, I try to avoid her whenever I can. She can be a real pain."

Cassidy rolled her eyes.

"If you see her, will you let us know?" the Coast Guardsman asked.

"Sure thing. Good luck."

A moment later, the boat's motor revved again,

and they started speeding through the water. But Jimmy James made no move to let Cassidy out of the storage space. She hoped it was because he was waiting until the coast was clear—literally.

But as her leg muscles began to tighten and cramp, flashbacks of being in the trunk of the car seized her.

Her lungs tightened until she could hardly breathe.

What if she was trapped down here?

Keep your cool, Cassidy.

But she couldn't. Panic filled her until she began thrashing in the small space.

She slammed her hand into the cover, hoping Jimmy James heard her over the hum of the motor.

A moment later, she heard a click. Felt movement. Fresh air surrounded her.

Jimmy James offered his hand to help her out.

"I had to wait until I was sure the Coast Guard was gone," he explained. "Are you okay?"

She bent over, trying to catch her breath. As hard as she tried, she couldn't get enough air into her lungs.

Calm down. You're not in the car. You're not trapped underwater.

A few breaths later, some of her panic began to

disappear. She straightened and let air fill her lungs one more time. Then she nodded.

"I'm fine," she said. "Thank you for covering for me. I'm sorry to put you in that position."

"It's okay. Now let's get to where we're going. It doesn't sound like we have any time to waste."

"*THAT'S* WHAT THIS IS ABOUT?" Watkins stared at Ty. "Your wife is in witness protection?"

Ty's spine remained stiff as he sat in his desk chair. "It's not officially witness protection but something similar. I wasn't going to say anything, but now that it's clear that Cassidy's life is in danger, I feel like I have no choice."

Watkins shifted his weight from one leg to another. "Why is she in witness protection?"

Ty took a deep breath before explaining the story to him.

Without invitation, Watkins sat in the chair across from Ty and shook his head. He almost looked deflated or maybe even stumped. "I've heard of her and what happened. I just had no idea . . ."

"Cassidy considered Samuel a close friend. She's

been grieving his death just like you have. She didn't do this to him."

"Then why was Samuel here? What about the messages on his phone?"

"We believe somebody is utilizing Alexandria Manchester's computer skills to plant evidence through technology. I don't believe that app was on Samuel's phone until somebody put it there after he died. Somebody wanted to make Cassidy look bad."

Watkins tapped his finger on the arm of the leather chair, his gaze intense with thought. "Why would somebody work this hard to make Cassidy appear guilty? Why focus on her?"

"They want to make sure that she stays quiet, for starters. Right before Samuel died, he muttered, 'They know.'"

Watkins' startled gaze shot toward Ty. "What does *that* mean?"

"We don't know for sure. But we do know that Alexandria Manchester found information on Cassidy that proved she used to be Cady Matthews. Alexandria—or the Shacklefords, I should say—told Governor Hollick that information about Cassidy, and they tried to blackmail the governor, to make him do something with Cassidy. If not, information about his own past misconduct would be spilled."

"What?" Watkins practically gawked at the information. "So you're saying the Shacklefords wanted to force Governor Hollick to take Cassidy down?"

Ty nodded. "We managed to hide most of those details." Ty knew he could be setting himself up to get in more trouble by admitting that, but he didn't have much choice at this point. "We had to protect Cassidy's identity."

Watkins grunted.

"But now somebody else knows information about who she is and wants to hold it against her. My personal theory is that Cassidy knows too much about what was going on with the Shacklefords."

"It sounds like you do too."

Ty's jaw tightened. He wanted to argue with the assessment, but he couldn't. "I fully expect to become the next target."

"And what does Annabeth have to do with any of this?"

"If these people have Annabeth, then they have control over her mother, Alexandria. With Alexandria's skills, she's a powerful weapon. They also have to know Cassidy would do anything to ensure the girl is returned safely."

Watkins didn't say anything for a minute.

"There's one more thing," Ty continued. "We

believe that assistant CIA director Gerald Mecklenburg might be involved." He filled him in on the details.

Ty waited, anxious to see what Watkins would say. He prayed he didn't regret sharing anything that he had. But he'd do whatever it took to protect Cassidy. He'd meant those words.

Included in that was trusting Watkins with sensitive information.

Could the special agent still be a bad guy?

Maybe.

But if he was, then he already knew these things.

And if he wasn't a bad guy, then sharing this information could help save Cassidy's life.

Now Ty just needed to wait to hear what Watkins was going to say.

This was the moment when Ty would see if this would pay off or if he'd end up in jail because of it.

CHAPTER FORTY

CASSIDY SPOTTED THE ISLAND AHEAD.

Some islands in this area were no more than raised areas of land big enough to park a few kayaks —oversized sandbars, essentially.

But Duck Island had marsh grass and several trees, making it one of the larger islands dotting the Pamlico. The lodge itself was probably three thousand square feet.

Currently, the sun set behind it. If only it was a little darker outside right now, it would work to their advantage.

But it wasn't.

"Slow down so they don't hear us coming," Cassidy told Jimmy James.

"Sure thing." Jimmy James shifted the boat into a lower gear.

There was nowhere to hide out here. They couldn't surprise anyone by skirting around trees or a building. An open expanse of water surrounded them.

Currently, no boats were docked outside the island—at least none that Cassidy could see from this side.

Still, Cassidy knew she needed to be careful here if she was going to rescue Annabeth.

Best-case scenario was that one person had been left to guard the girl. Cassidy could take that individual out, get Annabeth, and go.

Worst-case scenario was that these people were waiting for her. Cassidy was a fighter, but she had her limits. If she was too outnumbered . . .

Jimmy James puttered up to a dock and tied the boat to a post there. As he did, Cassidy climbed out, gripping her gun.

"Do you want me to go with you?" Jimmy James asked.

She looked back at him and shook her head. "I need you to stay here. If I find Annabeth, I need you to be waiting and ready to take off. Can you do that?"

Jimmy James tilted his head, as if her request

surprised him. "Whatever you want, Chief. But are you sure that you don't need backup?"

Cassidy wasn't sure about anything right now. "I'll yell if I need help."

He stared at her another moment before nodding. "I'll be here."

She silently sent her thanks. Then she hurried across the dock to the lodge in the distance. Cassidy tried to stay low so nobody would see her.

But she still didn't spot anyone.

Cassidy could be totally off base. Maybe Annabeth wasn't being kept here at all.

But this was her best guess, and she needed to check things out.

Soft on her feet, she climbed the steps toward the door. Staying against the wall, she peered inside the first window.

The living room stared back—the empty living room.

She continued around the wraparound deck, peering in windows.

From what she'd seen, no one was inside.

Finally, she went to the door and twisted the handle.

It was unlocked.

Quietly, she slipped inside.

Her gaze stopped at the stuffed teddy bear on the floor, just behind the couch.

Annabeth *had* been here.

Cassidy reached into her pocket to grab her phone.

But it was gone.

Gone? Where could it be?

Her breath caught.

When she climbed from the storage compartment in the boat, the device must have fallen out. She'd been so relieved to be free that she hadn't even thought to look for her cell phone.

Could that mistake end up costing her life?

She wouldn't be able to call Jimmy James, Ty, or any other backup.

Cassidy would have to take that risk. She didn't have time to think about that now.

Quickly, she worked her way around the rest of the house.

She opened every door. Every closet. Every cabinet.

But she didn't see Annabeth anywhere.

Cassidy paused in the living room, fighting back discouragement.

Was she too late?

Had these people taken her somewhere else?

And if so, where?

———

CASSIDY STOOD in the living room several minutes, trying to collect her thoughts and figure out her next plan of action.

She wouldn't leave this island until she was certain Annabeth wasn't here.

She tapped her foot against the carpeted floor.

Why would these people move Annabeth from this place?

They wouldn't, she realized. They had no reason to do that. Moving her from this island would mean they'd increase the likelihood she might be tracked down.

But if they left the girl here without a guard, they would need to feel confident she couldn't get away on her own.

Cassidy glanced around the lodge again with its deer heads and stuffed fish on the walls. An old boat mast with a halfway naked woman had been mounted over the fireplace.

This was definitely an overblown man cave of sorts.

But, based on the decorations, the original owner had also been quirky.

Could there be more here than meets the eye?

Cassidy already knew that nobody was in the house with her right now. She'd checked all the rooms.

Quickly, she walked to the window and scanned the outside again. The only person she spotted was Jimmy James as he waited on the boat.

With that reassurance, she yelled, "Annabeth?"

She waited.

Nothing.

Cassidy paced the rooms. "Annabeth? Can you hear me? It's Cassidy."

Still nothing.

She covered one side of the house before moving to the other.

Finally, near the fireplace, she heard a noise—a tapping.

Cassidy's breath caught. Where was that coming from?

"Annabeth?"

Something—or someone—had knocked on the wall.

Was there a secret room on the other side?

In an older house like this, it seemed like a possibility.

The idea was worth investigating.

Cassidy felt along the bookcase, tugging at various objects there.

There were no secret books. She hadn't really expected there to be.

But if there *was* a secret room, how would she get inside?

Finally, she pressed on the bookcase itself.

It was like a lever had flipped. The bookcase began to open—a spring latch had released.

Cassidy kept one hand on her gun just in case she needed to use it as she braced herself for what she might find inside.

CHAPTER FORTY-ONE

CASSIDY'S EYES widened as a figure came into sight. "Annabeth?"

"Cassidy!" The girl ran over and threw her arms around Cassidy.

Cassidy pulled Annabeth close, her heart brimming with love.

Annabeth was okay.

And she'd spoken.

Cassidy would have to revel in that fact later.

Right now, she needed to get out of here.

She leaned down and looked Annabeth in the eyes. She appeared clean and unharmed but . . . "Are you okay? Did they hurt you?"

Annabeth nibbled on her bottom lip a moment

before slowly saying, "I'm . . . okay. I knew you'd find me."

Cassidy glanced around the small, hidden room. There were several pillows on the floor, along with some blankets and a drawing pad. The space even had a small light.

She took Annabeth's hand and pulled her from the room. "We need to leave before these guys come back. We'll talk more as soon as I know you're safe."

Annabeth didn't say anything else as Cassidy pulled her through the house and outside. As soon as she stepped onto the porch, Cassidy scanned the island, looking for any signs of danger.

She didn't see anything.

"Jimmy James!" she yelled. "Get ready to go!"

He looked up from the boat and nodded.

Cassidy continued pulling Annabeth along, knowing they couldn't afford to slow down.

Finally, they reached the boat.

Jimmy James reached for Annabeth and helped the girl aboard.

As he did, Cassidy turned and saw a man rush onto the porch of the lodge.

He must have come from the other side of the island. It was the only way Cassidy wouldn't have seen him.

Her eyes widened when she saw the gun in his hands.

Cassidy rushed toward the boat when she heard someone shoot.

The next instant, pain pierced her shoulder.

She'd been shot.

She stepped toward the boat, desperate to climb inside.

But she couldn't.

Instead, she staggered backward.

She hit the water and sank, gasping as she tried to claw her way to the surface.

As her head bobbed up, she saw Jimmy James reach for her.

But there was no time for that.

That gunman would be here any moment.

"Go," she muttered. "Take Annabeth and get out of here. Now."

Then she sank back under the water.

TY DIALED Cassidy's number again.

And again, there was no answer.

He squeezed the phone in his hand, wondering what was going on.

What if she was in trouble?

Watkins was in a nearby office, also on the phone with someone.

Ty prayed that his risk paid off. But there were no certainties in life. Not when it came to things like this.

He only knew he had to find his wife.

His instincts told him she was in trouble, that she needed him right now.

Now that he'd laid everything out for Watkins, what did Ty have to hide?

There was only one thing he could think to do.

He hit the app he'd installed on the burner phone he'd given Cassidy and waited for it to load.

Then he blinked.

The map made it look like Cassidy was in the middle of the Pamlico Sound.

What sense did that make?

None, Ty realized. It didn't make *any* sense.

As he zoomed in, he saw there was an island there.

The infamous Duck Island. He'd heard many stories about the activities that went on at that place. Drinking. Women. Wild poker games.

Whenever Ty passed it, his chest tightened as if

his spirit was telling him that bad things happened there.

He was glad nobody had used the place in a long time because no good seemed to come from there.

So what was Cassidy doing there now?

He glanced across the hallway at Watkins. Should he even tell the man what was going on?

He needed to make a decision soon.

Because right now, Ty was going to gather his guys, and they were going to go find Cassidy.

CHAPTER FORTY-TWO

CASSIDY DESPERATELY TRIED to make it to the surface. But it seemed like no use. Her shoulder hurt too badly. She was losing blood. And she'd dropped her gun when she'd gone down.

Then, just as her head went under again, someone reached down and jerked her out of the water.

In one motion, she sprawled facedown on the dock, coughing water from her lungs and gasping in desperate breaths.

When she opened her eyes, she spotted Jimmy James zooming away from the shore in his boat.

With Annabeth.

At least the girl was safe.

For now.

Cassidy only hoped Jimmy James would be able to get Annabeth somewhere she could remain safe.

Cassidy flipped her head to the other side and saw two figures standing over her. She blinked several times, trying to get them to come into focus. But the pastels of sunset had turned into gray, and everything looked hazier than it should.

One was a man she had never seen before. Hired help, if she had to guess. Most likely the man who'd come into her home to supposedly check their cable.

And the other person was . . . a woman?

"Tina Andrews," Cassidy choked the words out as surprise captured her.

Of all the people on her radar, the reporter hadn't been one of them. Apparently, the woman wasn't really a reporter at all.

Cassidy should have seen through her.

But it was too late to reprimand herself for that now.

"You were supposed to die," Tina snarled as she stood above her.

Cassidy grasped her shoulder. She felt the warm blood still seeping from her wound. She felt herself growing weaker. Felt the world around her spinning.

"Sorry to disappoint you." Cassidy bit back the moan that wanted to escape.

"You're on your deathbed, yet you can still come up with a snarky reply. Good for you." Tina's eyebrows flickered up. "Since you're still alive, why don't you tell me where that phone is."

"What phone?"

"The one you stole from the Shacklefords. I know you have it."

Realization spread through her. "That's why you sent that imposter to the Blackout facility. He was looking for it, wasn't he?"

"Plus, it was good to have someone there keeping an eye on things." Tina snarled again. "Now where is it?"

"I don't have it. And if you wanted it so bad, why did you try to kill me?"

"We figured you were too much of a complication. It was time to cut our losses. Then we'd deal with the cell phone afterward."

"Well . . . I don't have it."

"Then I guess I'll just need to correct my past mistake and take care of you—once and for all."

"You're not going to get away with this." Cassidy met the woman's gaze.

Tina smirked. "I beg to differ. This is all going to look like your doing. We have it all planned. All the clues in place. You'll take the fall for this."

"Why?" Cassidy asked before drawing in another gasping breath of air. "I know you're working for Mecklenburg. I know he put you up to this. He doesn't want his secrets discovered. But I don't understand why you're focusing on me."

"Isn't it obvious?" Tina shook her head almost as if she pitied Cassidy. Then she nodded at her lackey. The man jerked Cassidy to her feet.

Pain ripped through her body. But Cassidy had no choice but to stand. The man wouldn't have it any other way.

"All the information the Shacklefords had was on the phone you guys stole from them. We need it back."

Cell phone that she stole? What were they talking about? "I don't have it. And that doesn't explain why you'd want to kill me."

"If you have the phone then you probably saw all the dirt the Shacklefords collected on Mecklenburg. That makes you too much of a risk."

The phone. Cassidy shook her head. She should have known. What *had* happened to that phone?

Mac had jammed the cell phone signal, but she had no idea where the device had disappeared to.

That meant that after these two were done with Cassidy, they would go after Ty too. She didn't have anything to hand over to them, and no amount of torture would change that.

The man shoved Cassidy forward.

"We need to take care of you once and for all," Tina said. "You're like the woman who won't die. But I'm about to change that."

With those words, Tina raised her gun.

Cassidy braced herself for the fight of her life.

"WHERE ARE YOU GOING?" Watkins asked behind him.

Ty stopped in his tracks in the hallway as he'd been heading toward the door. He turned around, anxious to get this conversation over with so he could get busy. "To find Cassidy. She's in trouble."

Watkins put his phone away and stepped closer. "How do you know? Did you talk to her?"

"No, she's not answering her phone."

"So . . . ?"

Ty shrugged, his impatience getting the best of him. "I don't know what else to tell you. She is. And I need to find her."

Watkins nodded before falling into step beside him. "I'm going with you."

"How do I know that I can trust you? That you won't turn around and arrest her?"

"I want to bring Mecklenburg down just as much as anybody. You were right. I looked into a few things, and he's crooked. The Shacklefords are going to help us out. Give their testimonies. I can't say they're going to have a reduced sentence because of it, but we're going to listen to them."

Ty stared at Watkins as he collected his thoughts. Finally, he nodded. "Okay then. You can come. But we need to go. Now."

Watkins nodded at two other men who were with him in the office.

Then they all rushed to the boat dock where Colton and Griff waited for them.

Just as their boat pulled away from the shore, Ty spotted a skiff coming toward them.

Ty squinted.

Was that . . . Jimmy James on board?

Ty looked at the tracker on the phone and saw that Cassidy's cell was getting closer to them.

Was she on the boat? Hope rose in him, but he reminded himself to be cautious.

As the boat came nearer, he spotted Jimmy James at the helm.

Someone was beside him, but this person was much smaller than Cassidy.

Was that . . . Annabeth?

His heart lurched into his throat.

Ty slowed his boat as Jimmy James pulled up beside him.

It *was* Annabeth! He wanted more than anything to hug her—but he couldn't reach her now. He could only hope his gaze conveyed how happy he was to see her.

"Annabeth . . ." he muttered.

She looked unharmed. That was great news.

"She's okay." Jimmy James nodded toward Annabeth. "But Cassidy . . . she needs your help."

"Where is she?"

"Duck Island."

"Duck Island?" Ty repeated.

Jimmy James nodded.

Ty looked back at Annabeth. "You and I will catch up in a little while. I've got to go help Cassidy now, okay?"

"Don't . . . let . . . those people . . . hurt her." Annabeth frowned as the words left her mouth.

Ty's lungs tightened as he heard the girl speak. She was talking! But he didn't have time to revel in that now.

Instead, he nodded, desperate to reassure Annabeth. "I'll do my best. Jimmy James, take Annabeth to Blackout and call Doc Clemson. Got it?"

"Got it." Jimmy James swallowed hard enough that his Adam's apple bobbed up and down. "Ty . . . Cassidy was shot. She told me to leave her. To get Annabeth to safety. But . . . it didn't look good."

Ty's breath caught.

Colton quickly zoomed away.

They had to get to Cassidy. Now.

CHAPTER FORTY-THREE

CASSIDY dug her heels into the sand beneath her, knowing she couldn't go any farther. She was just going to delay the inevitable.

They were going to kill her.

Why let them do that on their terms?

Instead, she tried to straighten her spine, despite the pain shooting through her. "You're not going to get away with this."

Tina smirked as she pointed the gun at Cassidy. "Watch me."

Using the last ounce of her strength, Cassidy swung her back leg around. The man behind her fell to his knees and into the water.

The move distracted Tina for a moment.

Using her good arm, Cassidy reached for the

woman's gun, shoving the barrel away from her chest. If Cassidy could gain control of the weapon, maybe she'd have a fighting chance to get out of this alive.

But Tina's grip on the gun was strong, and Cassidy's injured shoulder put her at a disadvantage.

Cassidy struggled to take the gun from her, but Tina swung the gun, slamming it into Cassidy's temple.

Her world began to spin.

The next instant, Tina shoved her. Her hand hit Cassidy's bullet wound.

Spots appeared in Cassidy's gaze as agony ripped through her muscles.

As Tina pinned Cassidy on the ground, more pain seared Cassidy's shoulder.

Tears popped into her eyes. Not from emotions. But because her body had never hurt like this before.

"Did you really think you were going to get away with that?" Tina growled on top of her.

Cassidy closed her eyes.

She couldn't give up. Not if she had any fight left inside her.

"Maybe." As Cassidy said the word, she rammed her elbow into Tina's throat.

The quick action knocked the wind out of the woman.

Tina's grip on the gun loosened, and the Glock flew across the ground.

Cassidy rolled Tina off her, then leapt to her feet.

She dove for the gun.

But Tina sprang from the ground. She lunged across the ground and her fingers wrapped around the handle.

As Cassidy dragged herself to her feet, she looked up.

Tina aimed the Glock at her.

Based on the look in the woman's eyes, she was ready to pull the trigger.

Dear Lord...

That was all Cassidy could manage to pray.

"KILL THE ENGINE," Ty told Colton as they got closer to the island. "And the lights."

The oversized sandbar was probably a hundred yards away. He saw someone on the shore. But Ty didn't want to alert whoever waited there.

Colton did as he asked, and they approached the island on the opposite side. As soon as they hit land, everyone dashed from the boat. Watkins and his men went one way, and Ty and his guys went the other.

Ty had seen the gun in that woman's hand.

Cassidy was only seconds away from possibly losing her life.

He darted through the sand, trying to reach Cassidy.

Dear Lord, be with us here. Keep her safe. I'm begging you.

Just as he reached the other side of the island, he saw Cassidy fall to her knees.

Had she been shot?

Ty's heart panged into his chest.

From somewhere deep inside him, a guttural, "No!" escaped.

CASSIDY'S KNEES FAILED HER, forcing her to drop to the ground.

Her head swam.

From pain?

From losing too much blood?

Both?

She didn't know.

She only knew she was losing the fight inside her. Her energy was waning.

And, if that happened, Tina would win.

She looked up again and drew in a breath.

Someone appeared in the distance behind Tina.

Cassidy gasped.

Was that . . . Watkins?

Was he here because he was a part of this scheme? Would Tina let him do the honor of killing Cassidy?

Her head continued to spin.

She was outnumbered. There was no way she could fight off both of them, especially in her current state.

At least Annabeth was safe.

That was the important thing.

Tina followed Cassidy's gaze and turned toward Watkins.

As she did, Watkins pulled the trigger.

Tina froze.

Two second later, she collapsed to the ground.

Cassidy held her breath as she watched, as she waited.

But Tina didn't move.

Was she dead?

Had Watkins just saved Cassidy's life?

She started to crumple to the ground.

But before she could, someone caught her elbows.

She looked up and saw . . .

"Ty?" she murmured.

Was she seeing things? How had he found her?

It didn't matter.

She'd never been so happy to see him.

CHAPTER FORTY-FOUR

THE FBI TOOK over the scene. As they did, Ty led Cassidy to steps climbing to the lodge. He seated her there to examine her injuries.

As he pulled shards of fabric away from her bullet wound, she winced. The good news was that the bleeding seemed to have slowed. She'd probably be okay, but she definitely needed to have this checked out.

However, her own injury was the last thing on her mind.

"Is Annabeth okay?" she rushed, searching his expression for the truth.

Ty nodded, reassurance filling his gaze. "Jimmy James took her to the Blackout campus. She was fine."

Air whooshed from Cassidy's lungs as relief filled her. She'd been so worried. "Thank goodness."

"I can't wait to hear the story of how Jimmy James got involved." Ty narrowed his gaze as he studied the wound.

"And I can't wait to tell you about it . . . later." Cassidy flinched as Ty touched the tender skin near the bullet's entry point.

"You're probably going to need surgery." He took off his outer shirt and pressed it into the injury. "But right now, we just need to stop the bleeding."

She flinched but didn't object. "I'm just happy to be alive."

Ty paused, and his gaze locked with hers. His voice cracked as he said, "I can't tell you how happy I am that you're still alive."

She squeezed his hand. "Please, tell me we don't have to stay here much longer."

"The Coast Guard should arrive at any time with their medic."

She closed her eyes, trying to ward away the wooziness she felt. She needed to remain lucid.

Her gaze wandered toward Watkins as he surveyed the scene near the dock. "I guess he's a good guy after all . . ."

"He saved your life, so I'd say so. But I had to tell

him the truth about your past. I'm sorry, but your life depended on it."

"I understand." Cassidy would have done the same thing in Ty's shoes. "But why didn't Samuel trust him?"

"Watkins and I talked about it as we headed to the island. My impression is that Watkins ran a background check on you after the incident with the Shacklefords. Samuel was afraid he'd start asking questions."

Ten minutes later, Cassidy leaned into Ty as they sat on the Coast Guard boat, headed back to Lantern Beach. He'd put a blanket over her and held her close—careful not to touch her injured shoulder.

Maybe this was all finally over.

Once she got to Blackout, Doc Clemson would be waiting to treat her at the clinic. Ty was right. She'd probably need surgery. She'd lost too much blood. The bullet may have hit muscle or bone.

Ty kissed the top of her forehead, not saying a word.

He didn't have to.

Cassidy had almost died twice today.

She'd been ready to leave this life if it had come down to it.

But she was so thankful none of those things had happened.

So, so thankful.

THE NEXT DAY, Cassidy was recovering from shoulder surgery at the Lantern Beach Medical Clinic.

She felt better, but she still hadn't seen Annabeth yet.

She needed to get herself together first. She didn't want to scar Annabeth any further by allowing the girl to see her in this state.

Skye and Lisa had stopped by to help Cassidy with her hair and makeup so she would look halfway normal.

Mac had also stopped by. He hadn't directly admitted to taking that cell phone the Shacklefords had been using. No doubt he didn't want to admit it. But the twinkle in his eyes indicated that he'd slipped it into his pocket before the FBI could grab it when the couple was arrested on that houseboat.

He hadn't wanted to risk the FBI finding any information on Cassidy.

She seriously owed that man her life.

Right now, Doc Clemson needed to finish checking her out so she could finally visit Annabeth.

"The bullet wound is looking good, Cassidy." He paused at the foot of her bed. "You're a very lucky woman. It could have done a lot more damage."

"I know. I'm pretty lucky too because I had the best care."

He brushed off his shoulder in fake modesty. "What can I say? But I want you be one of the first to know—I just hired a new doctor for the clinic."

Her eyes widened. "What? Are you retiring?"

"Nope. I'm just cutting back on my hours. I'm getting older, and I want to spend more time with Ernestine."

Ernestine was his reclusive girlfriend.

"Who's this new doctor?" Cassidy asked, curious about the newcomer.

"I think you'll like her. Name is Autumn Spenser. She's as smart as a whip."

"But you'll always be my doctor, right?"

He winked. "Of course. Now, as much as I'd like to chat with you more, you have someone outside anxiously waiting to see you."

Cassidy nodded and drew in a deep breath of anticipation. "Thank you. For everything."

"Of course." He smiled again before walking to the door and opening it.

As he did, Annabeth ran inside and stopped beside Cassidy's bed.

Ty trailed behind her, a grin on his face.

Cassidy reached over and squeezed the girl's hand. "Hey, sweetheart."

"Cassidy!"

Cassidy's heart pounded in her chest at the sound of Annabeth's voice. "It's so wonderful to hear your voice."

Annabeth just grinned and squeezed her hand tighter.

"How are you?" Cassidy turned her head toward the girl, careful to keep her shoulder still. It would be sore for a while but, with some physical therapy, it should soon be back to normal. "What have you and Ty been doing?"

"Puzzles. Games." Each word sounded animated and excited with a childhood wonder that was refreshing.

"That sounds like so much fun."

"Yes—fun! But I want you to play too."

"I've missed you too." Cassidy's voice dipped to a whisper as she tried to hold back her emotions.

"When can you come home?" Annabeth asked. "I want all three of us to take a walk with Kujo."

A bittersweet smile curled her lips. "Hopefully by tomorrow."

"Yay!"

Ty stepped closer, his eyes warm as he gazed at Cassidy "Are you feeling okay?"

"All things considered, I'm fine."

"Good. That's what I like to hear."

Watkins and his men had been in and out. They'd taken her statement. Given her updates. Written reports.

Watkins thought he had enough information to officially charge Mecklenburg. Last Cassidy had heard, he was on his way to do that now.

Getting that man out of office would do a favor to the world. Her lips curled with a touch of satisfaction at the thought. Justice had been served.

"We should probably let you rest," Ty said. "Your eyelids are drooping."

"I guess I am tired." She offered an apologetic smile.

"Even Supergirl needs to rest sometimes." Ty winked at her. "I'll come back and check on you later."

Annabeth leaned against Cassidy's arm, as if

giving her a half-hug. "I'm glad you're okay, Cassidy. Thank you . . ."

As Cassidy watched them walk away, her heart overflowed with love.

Things could have turned out so differently . . . but she was grateful that they hadn't.

She would treasure each day . . . because she realized more than ever that she wasn't promised tomorrow.

CHAPTER FORTY-FIVE

CASSIDY AND TY stood at the edge of their living room near the fireplace, with Gail and Kujo beside them. Annabeth twirled on the area rug in front of them as they waited for Alexandria to arrive.

Cassidy smiled as she watched the girl, who'd totally come out of her shell over the past three days since she'd been rescued.

She rubbed her arm, which was in a sling. It was desk duty for her for a while. But she was thankful to be alive.

Alexandria had been held at a secret CIA facility where Mecklenburg had placed her. He'd made her illegally hack into websites to find information online, utilizing her skills under the threat of hurting Annabeth.

It had been despicable, but at least he'd been caught and Alexandria had been released.

As the front door opened, Annabeth darted toward the woman who stepped inside. "Mommy!"

Alexandria scooped Annabeth up and folded her into her arms.

Tears sprang to Cassidy's eyes as she watched the reunion.

It had been a long journey to get here. But things finally appeared to be looking up.

Ty squeezed her waist, seeming to sense Cassidy felt more fragile than usual.

"I'm so glad she's okay," Gail murmured beside them.

Cassidy and Ty had given the social worker an update on what happened, and they'd gotten a good scolding in return—one they deserved. But by the grace of God, everything had turned out okay.

"Thank you both for stepping up and taking care of her." Gail hugged her clipboard to her chest as she continued to watch the reunion.

Cassidy smiled, the feeling bittersweet, especially as she realized that this was it. Annabeth would be leaving. Who knew when they'd see the girl again?

That realization left her with a hole in her heart.

"Of course," Cassidy finally muttered.

Alexandria took Annabeth's hand before walking toward them. "Yes, thank you all. Without you guys, I probably wouldn't be . . ." She didn't finish her statement as tears clouded her gaze.

But Cassidy knew what she was about to say.

Alexandria probably wouldn't be alive. Or she'd be alive but be a slave to Mecklenburg and his schemes.

"I'm glad we could be here." Ty's voice sounded tighter than usual, as if he were holding back his own grief.

"I'd love for you to keep in touch." Alexandria smiled as she watched Annabeth swing a toy rope around while Kujo tried to snatch it. "I mean, if you wouldn't mind . . ."

"We'd love that," Cassidy said. "We really would."

A grin spread across her face. "Wonderful. We'll arrange something soon then. In the meantime, I can't wait to take Annabeth to see her father."

"Joe?" Cassidy asked, uncertain if she'd understood correctly.

"He's awake. You didn't hear?"

Cassidy shook her head. "No, I didn't."

"He woke up two days ago, and he's been asking

to see us." Alexandria squeezed Annabeth's hand. "Special Agent Watkins is going to take us to the hospital to visit."

"That's great news," Cassidy said.

"Isn't it? Maybe life can finally return to something close to normal."

"I hope so. You all deserve it. I know you never intended on being pulled into any of this. You were just innocent bystanders."

In the past couple of days, Mecklenburg had been arrested. He was facing numerous charges, especially now that the Shacklefords were spilling everything they knew. Tina and her sidekick were in jail. Watkins had been hailed a hero.

Thank goodness, this was all over. Cassidy slept better knowing that.

A few minutes later, Gail said goodbye and left so she could get to work on another case.

Then it was time for Cassidy and Ty to say goodbye to Annabeth.

Cassidy dreaded this moment.

As they stood near the door, she leaned down to meet Annabeth eye to eye. She absently straightened the girl's collar. "I've really enjoyed having you here."

"I had fun." Annabeth twirled back and forth as if she were nervous.

"And I can't wait to see you again. It's almost summertime. Maybe you can come play at the beach sometime."

"Can we do that, Mommy? Please? Please?"

Alexandria took her hand. "I'd like that."

"And I'd love to beat you at UNO again." Ty winked at the girl.

Annabeth giggled. "I let you win!"

A moment passed. Suspended. Drawn out.

Cassidy wanted to deny that these events were going to play out. That Annabeth would really be gone.

But she couldn't do that.

Cassidy reached forward and pulled Annabeth into a long hug. Part of her felt like her heart was breaking. But she'd known this would most likely be the outcome.

As she pulled away, Ty reached down and embraced Annabeth.

Cassidy thought she saw tears in his eyes also.

When they finished embracing, Alexandria tugged Annabeth toward the door. Annabeth gave Kujo a long hug goodbye before stepping back.

With one last look and wave goodbye, the two of

them left.

As soon as the door closed, the house already felt more empty than it had before. No more UNO games or popcorn parties or tucking Annabeth in bed at night or silly cartoons playing on the TV in the background.

Ty turned to Cassidy as silence surrounded them. "Are you doing okay?"

Cassidy shrugged. "I guess. I'm going to miss Annabeth, though."

"Me too." He pulled her toward him and wrapped his arms around her, careful to avoid her sling.

She relished his embrace. But there was something she needed to tell him.

She couldn't put it off any longer.

"We need to talk," she told him softly.

Ty stepped back, concern in his gaze. "What's going on?"

Cassidy drew in a deep breath before starting. "As Clemson was prepping me for surgery, he had to do some tests. Just routine stuff."

"Okay . . . you're scaring me."

"Don't be scared." She squeezed his arm, trying to reassure him. "The truth is, in that process, I found out that I'm . . . pregnant."

His eyes widened. "What? But the doctor said . . ."

"I know what the doctor said. That I didn't produce enough eggs. But I guess I produced enough this time. I . . . I don't know. I don't have all the answers. But I had Doc Clemson double-check and even do an ultrasound."

Ty's voice dipped lower. "So we're really going to have a baby?"

Cassidy nodded, holding her breath as she waited for his reaction.

The next instant, Ty let out a whoop before lifting Cassidy off her feet and twirling her around. "I can't believe this. What great news."

"I can't believe it either."

He lowered her back to her feet and stared into her eyes, shock and thrill mingling in his gaze. "Even after everything that happened to you, everything you went through, the baby is still okay?"

"That was the first thing I asked also. Doc said the baby's fine."

Ty raked a hand through his hair before smiling. "I just can't believe this. When?"

"I'm due in seven months. We must have gotten pregnant right after our last visit with the fertility doctor. I've felt tired and nauseous, but I just thought it was everything we were going through."

He pushed a stray hair behind her ear. "You're going to be the best mom, Cassidy."

"And you're going to be the best dad. I really mean that. You were so great with Annabeth."

He leaned toward her and their lips met.

They still had a lot to figure out. More people knew Cassidy's real identity now. But she didn't think it mattered. DH-7 had fractured. The gang had other problems—bigger ones than Cassidy.

Maybe she *could* bring a child into this world without worrying every second that her past would ultimately hurt him or her.

Of course, Cassidy had all the normal new parent fears.

But she couldn't stop thanking God for this blessing.

For the moment, everything felt safe. Danger on the island had died down . . . for now.

And she was determined to enjoy the peace while it lasted.

She placed her hand on her belly. She still could hardly believe she was going to have a baby.

Life was about to change . . . and she couldn't wait.

COMING NEXT: ROCCO

Meet the New Blackout Recruits—starting with Rocco!

When nothing's as it seems, it's hard to know who to trust.

Former Navy SEAL and current Blackout recruit Rocco Foster thought his mission would be simple: figure out who's selling proprietary technology to the highest bidder and turn in the evidence. Things go south when an unsuspecting woman wanders into the middle of their operation.

Peyton Ellison likes to sprinkle happiness on those around her almost as much as she likes decorating the cupcakes she sells at her bakery. So why is someone targeting her and putting her life in danger?

Rocco is certain if he can figure out why someone set Peyton up that he can find answers. But first, he must keep her safe and earn her trust. Things get more complicated as peril continues to pummel them and incriminating evidence emerges.

Ultimately, Rocco and Peyton are both left with two questions: Who's telling the truth? And can the truth be trusted?

ALSO BY CHRISTY BARRITT:

LANTERN BEACH MYSTERIES

Hidden Currents

You can take the detective out of the investigation, but you can't take the investigator out of the detective. A notorious gang puts a bounty on Detective Cady Matthews's head after she takes down their leader, leaving her no choice but to hide until she can testify at trial. But her temporary home across the country on a remote North Carolina island isn't as peaceful as she initially thinks. Living under the new identity of Cassidy Livingston, she struggles to keep her investigative skills tucked away, especially after a body washes ashore. When local police bungle the murder investigation, she can't resist stepping in. But

Cassidy is supposed to be keeping a low profile. One wrong move could lead to both her discovery and her demise. Can she bring justice to the island . . . or will the hidden currents surrounding her pull her under for good?

Flood Watch

The tide is high, and so is the danger on Lantern Beach. Still in hiding after infiltrating a dangerous gang, Cassidy Livingston just has to make it a few more months before she can testify at trial and resume her old life. But trouble keeps finding her, and Cassidy is pulled into a local investigation after a man mysteriously disappears from the island she now calls home. A recurring nightmare from her time undercover only muddies things, as does a visit from the parents of her handsome ex-Navy SEAL neighbor. When a friend's life is threatened, Cassidy must make choices that put her on the verge of blowing her cover. With a flood watch on her emotions and her life in a tangle, will Cassidy find the truth? Or will her past finally drown her?

Storm Surge

A storm is brewing hundreds of miles away, but its effects are devastating even from afar. Laid-back, loose, and light: that's Cassidy Livingston's new motto. But when a makeshift boat with a bloody cloth inside washes ashore near her oceanfront home, her detective instincts shift into gear . . . again. Seeking clues isn't the only thing on her mind—romance is heating up with next-door neighbor and former Navy SEAL Ty Chambers as well. Her heart wants the love and stability she's longed for her entire life. But her hidden identity only leads to a tidal wave of turbulence. As more answers emerge about the boat, the danger around her rises, creating a treacherous swell that threatens to reveal her past. Can Cassidy mind her own business, or will the storm surge of violence and corruption that has washed ashore on Lantern Beach leave her life in wreckage?

Dangerous Waters

Danger lurks on the horizon, leaving only two choices: find shelter or flee. Cassidy Livingston's new identity has begun to feel as comfortable as her favorite sweater. She's been tucked away on Lantern Beach for weeks, waiting to testify against a deadly gang, and is settling in to a new life she wants to last forever. When she thinks she spots someone malevolent from her past, panic swells inside her. If an enemy has found her, Cassidy won't be the only one who's a target. Everyone she's come to love will also be at risk. Dangerous waters threaten to pull her into an overpowering chasm she may never escape. Can Cassidy survive what lies ahead? Or has the tide fatally turned against her?

Perilous Riptide

Just when the current seems safer, an unseen danger emerges and threatens to destroy everything. When Cassidy Livingston finds a journal hidden deep in the recesses of her ice cream truck, her curiosity kicks into high gear. Islanders suspect that Elsa, the journal's owner, didn't die accidentally. Her final entry indicates their suspicions might be correct and that what Elsa observed on her final night may have led to her demise. Against the advice of Ty Chambers, her former Navy SEAL boyfriend, Cassidy taps into her detective skills and hunts for answers. But her search only leads to a skeletal body and trouble for both of them. As helplessness threatens to drown her, Cassidy is desperate to turn back time. Can Cassidy find what she needs to navigate the perilous situation? Or will the riptide surrounding her threaten everyone and everything Cassidy loves?

Deadly Undertow

The current's fatal pull is powerful, but so is one detective's will to live. When someone from Cassidy Livingston's past shows up on Lantern Beach and warns her of impending peril, opposing currents collide, threatening to drag her under. Running would be easy. But leaving would break her heart. Cassidy must decipher between the truth and lies, between reality and deception. Even more importantly, she must decide whom to trust and whom to fear. Her life depends on it. As danger rises and answers surface, everything Cassidy thought she knew is tested. In order to survive, Cassidy must take drastic measures and end the battle against the ruthless gang DH-7 once and for all. But if her final mission fails, the consequences will be as deadly as the raging undertow.

LANTERN BEACH ROMANTIC SUSPENSE

Tides of Deception

Change has come to Lantern Beach: a new police chief, a new season, and . . . a new romance? Austin Brooks has loved Skye Lavinia from the moment they met, but the walls she keeps around her seem impenetrable. Skye knows Austin is the best thing to ever happen to her. Yet she also knows that if he learns the truth about her past, he'd be a fool not to run. A chance encounter brings secrets bubbling to the surface, and danger soon follows. Are the life-threatening events plaguing them really accidents . . . or is someone trying to send a deadly message? With the tides on Lantern Beach come deception and lies. One question remains—who will be swept away as the water shifts? And will it bring the end for Austin and Skye, or merely the beginning?

Shadow of Intrigue

For her entire life, Lisa Garth has felt like a supporting character in the drama of life. The designation never bothered her—until now. Lantern Beach, where she's settled and runs a popular restaurant, has boarded up for the season. The slower pace leaves her with too much time alone. Braden Dillinger came to Lantern Beach to try to heal. The former Special Forces officer returned from battle with invisible scars and diminished hope. But his recovery is hampered by the fact that an unknown enemy is trying to kill him. From the moment Lisa and Braden meet, danger ignites around them, and both are drawn into a web of intrigue that turns their lives upside down. As shadows creep in, will Lisa and Braden be able to shine a light on the peril around them? Or will the encroaching darkness turn their worst nightmares into reality?

Storm of Doubt

A pastor who's lost faith in God. A romance writer who's lost faith in love. A faceless man with a deadly obsession. Nothing has felt right in Pastor Jack Wilson's world since his wife died two years ago. He hoped coming to Lantern Beach might help soothe the ragged edges of his soul. Instead, he feels more alone than ever. Novelist Juliette Grace came to the island to hide away. Though her professional life has never been better, her personal life has imploded. Her husband left her and a stalker's threats have grown more and more dangerous. When Jack saves Juliette from an attack, he sees the terror in her gaze and knows he must protect her. But when danger strikes again, will Jack be able to keep her safe? Or will the approaching storm prove too strong to withstand?

Winds of Danger

Wes O'Neill is perfectly content to hang with his friends and enjoy island life on Lantern Beach.

Something begins to change inside him when Paige Henderson sweeps into his life. But the beautiful newcomer is hiding painful secrets beneath her cheerful facade. Police dispatcher Paige Henderson came to Lantern Beach riddled with guilt and uncertainties after the fallout of a bad relationship. When she meets Wes, she begins to open up to the possibility of love again. But there's something Wes isn't telling her—something that could change everything. As the winds shift, doubts seep into Paige's mind. Can Paige and Wes trust each other, even as the currents work against them? Or is trouble from the past too much to overcome?

Rains of Remorse

A stranger invades her home, leaving Rebecca Jarvis terrified. Above all, she must protect the baby growing inside her. Since her estranged husband died suspiciously six months earlier, Rebecca has been determined to depend on no one but herself. Her chivalrous new neighbor appears to be an answer to prayer. But who is Levi Stoneman really? Rebecca wants to believe he can help her, but she can't ignore her instincts. As danger closes in, both Rebecca and Levi must figure out whom they can trust. With Rebecca's baby coming soon, there's no time to waste. Can the truth prevail . . . or will remorse overpower the best of intentions?

Torrents of Fear

The woman lingering in the crowd can't be Allison . . . can she? Because Allison was pronounced dead six years ago. Musician Carter Denver knows only one person who's capable of helping him find answers: Sadie Thompson, his estranged best friend and someone who also knew Allison. He needs to know if he's losing his mind or if Allison could have survived her car accident. Could Allison really be alive? If so, why is she trying to harm Carter and Sadie? As the two try to find answers, can Sadie keep her feelings for Carter hidden? Could he ever care for her, or is the man of her dreams still in love with the woman now causing his nightmares?

LANTERN BEACH PD

On the Lookout

When Cassidy Chambers accepted the job as police chief on Lantern Beach, she knew the island had its secrets. But a suspicious death with potentially far-reaching implications will test all her skills

—and threaten to reveal her true identity. Cassidy enlists the help of her husband, former Navy SEAL Ty Chambers. As they dig for answers, both uncover parts of their pasts that are best left buried. Not everything is as it seems, and they must figure out if their John Doe is connected to the secretive group that has moved onto the island. As facts materialize, danger on the island grows. Can Cassidy and Ty discover the truth about the shadowy crimes in their cozy community? Or has darkness permanently invaded their beloved Lantern Beach?

Attempt to Locate

A fun girls' night out turns into a nightmare when armed robbers barge into the store where Cassidy and her friends are shopping. As the situation escalates and the men escape, a massive manhunt launches on Lantern Beach to apprehend the dangerous trio. In the midst of the chaos, a potential foe asks for Cassidy's help. He needs to find his sister who fled from the secretive Gilead's Cove community on the island. But the more Cassidy learns about the seemingly untouchable group, the more her unease grows. The pressure to solve both cases continues to mount. But as the gravity of the situation rises, so does the danger. Cassidy is determined to protect the island and break up the cult . . . but doing so might cost her everything.

First Degree Murder

Police Chief Cassidy Chambers longs for a break from the recent crimes plaguing Lantern Beach. She simply wants to enjoy her friends' upcoming wedding, to prepare for the busy tourist season about to slam the island, and to gather all the dirt she can on the suspicious community that's invaded the town. But trouble explodes on the island, sending residents—including Cassidy—into a squall of uneasiness. Cassidy may have more than one enemy plotting her demise, and the collateral damage seems unthinkable. As the temperature rises, so does the pressure to find answers. Someone is determined that Lantern Beach would be better off without their new police chief. And for Cassidy, one wrong move could mean certain death.

Dead on Arrival

With a highly charged local election consuming the community, Police Chief Cassidy Chambers braces herself for a challenging day of breaking up petty conflicts and tamping down high emotions. But when widespread food poisoning spreads among potential voters across the island, Cassidy smells something rotten in the air. As Cassidy examines every possibility to uncover what's going on, local enigma Anthony Gilead again comes on her radar. The man is running for mayor and his cult-like following is growing at an alarming rate. Cassidy feels certain he has a spy embedded in her inner circle. The problem is that her pool of suspects gets deeper every day. Can Cassidy get to the bottom of what's eating away at her peaceful island home? Will voters turn out despite the outbreak of illness plaguing their tranquil town? And the even bigger question: Has darkness come to stay on Lantern Beach?

Plan of Action

A missing Navy SEAL. Danger at the boiling point. The ultimate showdown. When Police Chief Cassidy Chambers' husband, Ty, disappears, her world is turned upside down. His truck is discovered with blood inside, crashed in a ditch on Lantern Beach, but he's nowhere to be found. As they launch a manhunt to find him, Cassidy discovers that someone on the island has a deadly obsession with Ty. Meanwhile, Gilead's Cove seems to be imploding. As danger heightens, federal law enforcement officials are called in. The cult's growing threat could lead to the pinnacle standoff of good versus evil. A clear plan of action is needed or the results will be devastating. Will Cassidy find Ty in time, or will she face a gut-wrenching loss? Will Anthony Gilead finally be unmasked for who he really is and be brought to justice? Hundreds of innocent lives are at stake . . . and not everyone will come out alive.

LANTERN BEACH BLACKOUT

Dark Water

Colton Locke can't forget the black op that went terribly wrong. Desperate for a new start, he moves to Lantern Beach, North Carolina, and forms Blackout, a private security firm. Despite his hero status, he can't erase the mistakes he's made. For the past year, Elise Oliver hasn't been able to shake the feeling that there's more to her husband's death than she was told. When she finds a hidden box of his personal possessions, more questions—and suspicions—arise. The only person she trusts to help her is her husband's best friend, Colton Locke. Someone wants Elise dead. Is it because she knows too much? Or is it to keep her from finding the truth? The Blackout team must uncover dark secrets hiding beneath seemingly still waters. But those very secrets might just tear the team apart.

Safe Harbor

Guilt over past mistakes haunts former Navy SEAL Dez Rodriguez. When he's asked to guard a pop star during a music festival on Lantern Beach, he's all set for what he hopes is a breezy assignment. Bree hasn't found fame to be nearly as fulfilling as she dreamed. Instead, she's more like a carefully crafted character living out a pre-scripted story. When a stalker's threats become deadly, her life—and career—are turned upside down. From the start, Bree sees her temporary bodyguard as a player, and Dez sees Bree as a spoiled rich girl. But when they're thrown together in a fight for survival, both must learn to trust. Can Dez protect Bree—and his carefully guarded heart? Or will their safe harbor ultimately become their death trap?

Ripple Effect

Griff McIntyre never expected his ex-wife and three-year-old daughter to come to Lantern Beach. After an abduction attempt, they're desperate for safety. Now Griff's not letting either of them out of his sight. Bethany knows Griff is the only one who can protect them, despite the fact that he broke her heart. But she'll do anything to keep her daughter safe—even if it means playing nicely with a man she can't stand. As peril ripples through their lives, Griff and Bethany must work together to protect their daughter. But an unseen enemy wants something from them . . . and will stop at nothing to get it. When disaster strikes, can Griff keep his family safe? Or will past mistakes bring the ultimate failure?

Rising Tide

Benjamin James knows there's a traitor within his former command. The rest of his team might even think it's him. As danger closes in, he must clear himself and stop a deadly plot by a dangerous terrorist group. All CJ Compton wanted was a new start after her career ended under suspicion. Working as the house manager for private security group Blackout seems perfect. But there's more trouble here than what she left behind. As the tide rushes in, the stakes continue to rise. If the Blackout team fails, it's not just Lantern Beach at stake—it's the whole country. Can Benjamin and CJ overcome their differences and work together to find the truth?

USA Today has called Christy Barritt's books "scary, funny, passionate, and quirky."

Christy writes both mystery and romantic suspense novels that are clean with underlying messages of faith. Her books have won the Daphne du Maurier Award for Excellence in Suspense and Mystery, have been twice nominated for the Romantic Times Reviewers' Choice Award, and have finaled for both a Carol Award and Foreword Magazine's Book of the Year.

She is married to her Prince Charming, a man who thinks she's hilarious—but only when she's not trying to be. Christy is a self-proclaimed klutz, an avid music lover who's known for spontaneously bursting into song, and a road trip aficionado.

When she's not working or spending time with her family, she enjoys singing, playing the guitar, and exploring small, unsuspecting towns where people have no idea how accident-prone she is.

Find Christy online at:
    www.christybarritt.com
    www.facebook.com/christybarritt
    www.twitter.com/cbarritt

Sign up for Christy's newsletter to get information on all of her latest releases here: **www. christybarritt.com/newsletter-sign-up/**

If you enjoyed this book, please consider leaving a review.